The New Amish Girl

Amish Foster Girls Book 3

Samantha Price

Chapter 1.

Be strong and of a good courage,
fear not, nor be afraid of them: for the LORD thy
God,
he it is that doth go with thee; he will not fail thee,
nor forsake thee.
Deuteronomy 31:6

"My niece Stephanie is coming to stay with us for a few months."

That was the first time Megan had heard of *Mamm* Gretchen's *Englisch* niece in over two years and that was most likely because Stephanie's father was an outcast. Her father was Gretchen's brother, who had left the Amish when he was a teenager and had never returned.

"Why is she coming?" It was a perfectly simple question and Megan expected the answer to be just as simple.

"Just because," was the answer her foster mother, Gretchen Graber, gave her.

Simple, Megan thought, *but entirely uninformative.*

Megan was one of the two remaining foster children at the Grabers, since the third, Elizabeth, had recently gotten married.

"Well, when's she coming?" Surely *Mamm* Gretchen would tell her that much.

"Today."

"So soon?"

Her foster mother nodded and her lips remained closed.

"Aren't you going to tell me why she's coming here?"

Momentarily ignoring Megan's question, Gretchen looked around the corner of the kitchen into the living room. When Megan peeped around too, she saw that Gretchen was looking at her husband who was reading The Bulletin, an Amish newspaper.

Gretchen ushered Megan to the back of the kitchen and whispered in her ear, "She's gotten into a lot of trouble and Tom thinks she needs time with the community to sort her life out."

Megan searched Gretchen's face. "What kind of trouble?"

Gretchen shook her head so hard that her bottom lip wobbled. "Never mind about that."

"I won't tell anyone." Megan knew, with just a little encouragement Gretchen would reveal all.

"Well, you'll have to pretend you don't know." Gretchen eyed her skeptically.

"Of course. I won't tell anyone anything. I'll pretend I don't know a thing—not one thing."

"She was involved in stealing a large sum of money. The court let her go since it was her first offense, and it helped that Tom told the officials he would have her come here for a time."

Megan tapped a finger on her chin. She figured Gretchen's brother, Tom, did not think that the stay in the Amish community would do her good, but rather, the court might have enforced her stay. As always, Megan's thoughts wandered to Brandon. Megan wondered what Stephanie might steal of hers. It didn't really matter as long as she did not take Brandon. Megan smiled knowing no one would be able to steal him. Anyway, he wasn't even hers—not yet.

"Why are you smiling? Are you looking forward to having another girl in the *haus* since Elizabeth's gone?"

"*Jah*, that's it. It'll be nice having another girl around especially with Tara at work most days and spending the rest of her time with Caleb."

"You must be on your best behavior while she's here. Understood?"

Megan nodded, a little offended at *Mamm* Gretchen thinking that she was ever on anything less than her best behavior.

That afternoon a car pulled up outside the house and then Tom and Stephanie stepped out. Megan watched them out the kitchen window. Stephanie was still beautiful; it didn't take Megan long to notice that. She was fancy and wore fancy clothes and makeup. Megan had to wonder if she'd still look that good with the makeup scrubbed off and dressed in plain Amish clothing.

Mamm Gretchen walked into the house carrying Stephanie's small suitcase while *Dat* William and Tom spoke to each other at Tom's car.

"Stephanie." Megan walked over to Stephanie and gave her a hug, as soon as she walked into the house.

"Hi, Megan."

Stephanie seemed much quieter than Megan remembered. Maybe she was embarrassed at being shuffled away somewhere, hidden amongst their Amish community. Or, maybe she was ashamed over her wrongdoing and humiliated that she'd been arrested.

William came inside after Tom had driven away. "Nice to have you here, Stephanie. You can stay as long as you like."

"Thank you, Uncle William."

Stephanie sounded so sweet that Megan wondered if she was innocent of the crime she'd been accused of. She couldn't wait to get Stephanie alone to find out exactly what had gone on.

William said to Gretchen, "I've just got a few errands to run and then I've got work waiting down the end of the farm."

Gretchen nodded, not saying a word to her husband, and as William walked out the door, her attention turned to Stephanie's clothes. "We'll have to find you something suitable to wear."

By 'we' Megan knew that Gretchen meant that she'd have to do it. "Come with me, Stephanie," Megan said before Gretchen had the time to ask. "We've plenty of dresses upstairs." Megan picked up Stephanie's suitcase and Stephanie followed her up the stairs.

Megan walked into Elizabeth's old room. "You'll be staying in this room."

"I stayed in this room with Elizabeth last time I was here. I heard she got married just recently."

"She did." Megan pointed to some dresses hanging on the clothes pegs. "They're freshly washed and they should fit you."

Stephanie pulled a face. "Do I really have to wear one of them?"

Megan smiled. "I would if I were you. You know how strict Gretchen and William are. If they ask you to do something, it's a lot easier to do it the first time 'round. They'll always win in the end." Megan passed a yellow dress to Stephanie.

Stephanie took it and held it out at arm's length. "You've got to be kidding me."

Megan giggled. "You'll have to get used to it. Don't worry; everyone wears the same, so it doesn't really matter." Megan studied Stephanie's heavily made up face. "And, sooner or later, Gretchen will ask you to wash your face."

"Oh yeah, the makeup?"

Megan nodded.

"It just gets worse." Stephanie rubbed her head.

Megan sat on the bed. "So what did you do that was so bad?"

With dress in hand, Stephanie sat next to her. "I guess I just got mixed up with some bad people. I thought they were my friends, but when they got questioned it seemed they all blamed me, or one of them did at least."

Megan wondered if anyone was really 'bad.' Now it appeared that Stephanie carried that label just because of one mistake. "Is Gretchen supposed to straighten you out?"

"I guess so." Stephanie threw herself back on the bed and stared up at the ceiling. "What's there to do around here?"

"Chores. Nothing's changed since you were here last."

"I thought so."

Megan was glad that Stephanie was easy to speak with. She'd have a friend while she was staying there.

"Megan, why are you here? How did you come to be here?"

"Well…"

"You don't have to tell me if you don't want to."

"It's okay. I don't mind talking about it. My father died when I was a baby and my mother got very sick and had to give me up. There was no one to look after either of us. No family at all. I don't know what became of my mother after that, but she never came looking for me. My best guess is that she died."

"I'm sorry, Megan. Where did you go when you were a baby? I know you've only been with Gretchen and William for a few years."

"I went from foster home to foster home. I was a sickly child. I don't remember that part, but that's what I've been told. Some of the places I lived in weren't the best. I love it here. This is the only home I've ever truly had."

"I guess I should be grateful for my parents. Mostly I'm just annoyed with them. Now down to the important things. Are there any men around?"

"There are a few who have started visiting recently, but none that I really like. They mostly end up talking to Gretchen. I find it hard to know what to say to them."

"I was talking about for myself." Stephanie giggled. "Anyway, why do you let them talk to Gretchen when they come here?"

"I just don't know what to say."

"I get like that too sometimes. Where can we go to find some men?"

"You want to see Amish men?"

Stephanie nodded.

"Amish men wouldn't be allowed to date *Englisch* girls."

Stephanie smiled widely and tossed the dress in the air. "Well, they won't know because I'll be wearing this." She caught the dress and held it toward Megan who ignored her comments.

On the one hand, she did not want Stephanie to lead any Amish boys astray. On the other, it might be good for her to have an Amish boyfriend to steer her in the right direction. "I'll find you some boots that should fit you."

When Megan came back into Stephanie's room, she had two pairs of boots in her hands. "Here, I've found these. They're slightly different sizes, so one pair should fit. I'll go down and see if *Mamm* needs any help with dinner. Come to the kitchen when you're ready."

"Thanks, Megan."

Here I am, stuck in this place as if I'm in a time warp, Stephanie thought. *I don't even have my cell or my computer.*

Looking around at the bleak room, she pulled a face. Apart from the blue and green quilt on the bed, the room was entirely a bland shade of gray. Nothing was in the room that didn't have a purpose. There were no ornaments, no paintings or posters on the walls—nothing, not so much as a mirror. A bed, a dresser, and a nightstand were all the furniture in the room. She flung herself back and looked up at the ceiling again.

Okay. The bed's comfortable. I suppose that's something.

Stephanie got off the bed and when she pulled the plain gray curtains apart to look out the window, she saw nothing but farmland for miles. The snow had melted away and the low afternoon sun shining through the leafless branches of the trees created shafts of light beyond the barn. It was a pretty sight, but Stephanie would've preferred to be closer to the action. And that meant near a coffee shop.

Looking out to nothingness in the faraway fields, she thought, *Where am I going to get my double caramel lattes from?* She was a city girl at heart.

There wasn't a coffee shop within miles. At home where she lived with her parents, the local coffee shop was a short walk. There she'd meet up with her friends every day. When she'd been living away from home recently, she'd been living above a store in the middle of town and had her choice of cafés.

11

"Now I'm here in the middle of nowhere!" she mumbled to herself.

She wondered what kind of coffee they served in jail. *Most likely instant coffee. Yuck!* Her mood worsened when she suddenly realized tomorrow was Sunday.

With my luck, it'll be the second Sunday, the Sunday that their church gathering falls.

Stephanie had attended a Sunday meeting when she had stayed with them last time. What stood out in her mind was that the wooden bench seats were hard, and that the men and women sat on different sides of the room. Perhaps she might see Jared Weaver again, unless he'd moved away, or worse, she might learn that he had gotten married.

The only good thing about the Amish church meetings was all the food there was when the service was over. Now that she was watching her figure, she was trying to be less interested in food, but who would notice a few more pounds under the horrid dresses she'd be wearing for the next few months?

Stephanie let go of the curtains and they fell closed, causing the room to once again become gloomy and darkened. She slipped off her jeans and tee shirt and pulled on the purple Amish dress instead of the yellow one Megan had handed to her, and then the traditional black stockings. Lastly, she pushed her feet into one of the pairs of black lace-up boots that Megan had brought to her. She hoped that they would not make her wear a prayer *kapp* like all the other women did since she wasn't really Amish. Stephanie went down to join her aunt and Megan in the kitchen.

* * *

As Stephanie helped Megan and Aunt Gretchen in the kitchen, Gretchen handed her cutlery to set the table. As she laid it out, she said, "I thought you said Tara wasn't coming home for dinner?"

"She's not," Megan answered.

"So, I only set... Let me see. There's us three and Uncle William, so that's four of us for dinner and you've given me five of everything."

"That's right. We've got a farm hand who eats with us. He sleeps in a room off from the barn," Megan said.

"He's a nice young man. His name's Jared Weaver," Gretchen said as she got the dinner plates out of the cupboard.

Stephanie froze, clutching the cutlery in her hand. "Jared Weaver?"

Gretchen looked up. "*Jah.* Do you know him?"

"Um. I might remember him from last time I was here. Or maybe not, maybe the name just sounded familiar." She carried on with setting the table, trying to stop herself from smiling too much. Maybe her stay here wouldn't be so bad after all. *He can't be married, not if he's staying in a room off from the barn. There was no mention of a wife.*

Darkness fell and William and Jared came home. William walked in the door first and then Jared walked into the kitchen. He was every bit as nice-looking as Stephanie remembered him. His hair was thick and dark, with eyes an unusual shade of dark hazel.

"Hello, Stephanie."

He remembered my name! "Hello, Jared."

"You two know each other?" Uncle William asked looking directly at Stephanie.

"We met a couple of years ago," Jared said, smiling at Stephanie.

After they'd taken their seats around the dining table, they closed their eyes to give their silent thanks for the food set before them.

Megan opened one eye and saw that Stephanie had her eyes closed too.

Once they were finished with their prayers, William said, "So we've got the gathering tomorrow, Stephanie."

Stephanie nodded smiling all the while. Megan noticed Stephanie's gaze kept veering toward Jared.

William continued, "You don't have to go if you'd rather stay here."

Megan could not believe what he'd just said, and she stared at him in disbelief. Why was he letting

Stephanie off going to the meeting? Didn't she have to live as one of them while she was there? Otherwise, what was the point? Last time she was there Stephanie had to go to all their Amish events including the meetings.

"No that's all right. I'd like to go," Stephanie said.

Megan then transferred her open-mouthed stare toward Stephanie until her foster mother tapped her foot under the table.

"You would really like to go?" Megan asked Stephanie, figuring it might have something to do with Jared.

Stephanie nodded while she spooned food onto her plate from one of the bowls in the center of the table.

The dinner was spent in awkward silence. No one could ask Stephanie what she'd been up to, or about school because she'd dropped out.

"We've got bees now, Stephanie." Megan interrupted the silence with her statement.

Jared laughed. "You and your bees, Megan."

"Don't laugh, Jared. They're very interesting."

"As long as they keep away from me and don't bite me, I suppose they're okay," Jared said.

"They've never stung you yet, have they?"

"*Nee*, they must be friendly bees."

15

"You won't mind so much when you're putting their honey on your bread."

"That's true," Jared said.

Stephanie turned to Megan. "So you keep bees, with a queen bee, a hive and everything?"

Megan nodded enthusiastically. "I've got a few hives, in fact, and in the summertime, the man who gave them to me said I'd get enough honey to sell. We'll have more than we can eat. I can show you the hives tomorrow."

William coughed loudly.

Glancing at William's stern face, Megan corrected herself. "Well, tomorrow after the meeting we might have some time. That is if we don't stay on for the young people's singing."

"I'd like that. I've never seen bees' hives before." Stephanie shoveled mashed potato onto her fork.

That night, Megan sat up sewing and wondering what man in the community would be a suitable match for Stephanie. Surely if Stephanie became a part of their community, she'd keep out of trouble. And what better way of doing that than to find her a suitable man? She would keep close to Stephanie tomorrow, and then she would test her matchmaking skills.

16

Chapter 2.

But they that wait upon the LORD shall renew their strength;
they shall mount up with wings as eagles;
they shall run, and not be weary;
and they shall walk, and not faint.
Isaiah 40:31

Stephanie did not know whether it was being away from her family and friends or being with her Amish aunt and uncle, but she was thinking about God for the first time in ages.

Even though her father had left the Amish, he believed in God. Her parents had sent her to Sunday School when she was younger, and, despite Stephanie seldom joining them anymore, they regularly attended church together. Stephanie knew that she should pray a prayer of forgiveness. Staying with her aunt and uncle, there seemed no getting away from God.

Dear God, forgive me for all the bad things I've done and all the people who I've hurt. Please lead me and guide me to have a good life. I don't want to make any mistakes anymore. I want to lead a good and happy life. Amen.

Stephanie wasn't sure what she should have prayed, but she remembered that someone once said that if you're pure in your heart, God hears your prayer. She closed her eyes and for the first time in a long time fell asleep quickly, peacefully.

When Tara came home from spending time with Caleb, Megan waved her over as she stepped in the door.

Tara flopped on the couch next to her.

"Stephanie's here. *Mamm's* niece."

"Already? I thought she wasn't coming until Monday."

"You knew she was coming?"

"*Jah.*"

"*Mamm* didn't tell me until this morning just before she arrived."

"She told me over breakfast just before I left this morning. I wasn't listening properly. Obviously, she must have said she was coming today."

"Oh."

"How much do you know about her?" Tara asked.

Megan said, "All *Mamm* told me was that she'd gotten into trouble and Tom asked the courts if she could come here."

"Yeah, that's what I heard."

"You remember her from a couple of years ago, don't you?" Megan asked.

"I do, but what's she like now?"

"Pretty much the same. I thought she might be interested in Jared since they seemed to get on so well over dinner, but she didn't ask me one thing about him. She did ask me where all the men are, so she's interested in men."

Tara giggled. "Aren't we all?"

Megan pulled a face.

"Except you of course."

"I guess."

"You only like Brandon."

Megan frowned. She wasn't sure that she should be talking to Brandon's half sister about her feelings for him.

"Why don't you come with me on Tuesday night? Brandon will be there."

Every Tuesday night, Tara had dinner with her newfound birth family — her father, her younger sister, and her half-brother, Brandon. Megan had been with Tara at the first dinner and had met Brandon and they'd hit it off right away. Megan was painfully shy with other men, but with Brandon, it was somehow different.

"What about Caleb?" Megan asked. "Doesn't he want to go with you this time?"

"He doesn't have to. He's been the last few times."

"Yeah, I know."

Tara leaned in towards her. "Well?"

"*Jah*, I'd like to go. *Denke.*"

"Good! That's settled, then."

19

Megan hushed Tara. "You don't want to wake anyone up. How are things with Caleb?"

"What do you mean?"

"Are you sure he doesn't mind waiting to marry you?"

"He agreed to it, and I'm not ready yet."

"Hmmm." Megan frowned at her.

"What was that for? You sound like Gretchen when you do that," Tara said.

"Are you sure you're over Mark?"

"Do you think that's why I'm not rushing into marrying Caleb?"

"Don't get angry, but I thought it might have something to do with it."

Tara shook her head. "I'm not angry. I just don't see how you could think I would still have any feelings for Mark at all after what he's been like."

Megan shrugged. "You liked him once."

"Jah, well that was a big mistake. And now he's already marrying Mary Lou after telling me, I don't know how many times, that they were only friends. He was stringing Mary Lou and me along, probably seeing which one would say yes to him first."

"You can't say that for certain."

Tara shrugged. "It's pretty obvious."

"When are they getting married? Have you heard?"

"It'll be at the end of the year. I think someone said November."

"That's a long time to wait."

"I just hope Mark doesn't change his mind. It would break Mary Lou's heart, but that's what type of person he is."

"Yeah, I'd hate to see that happen. I think she's a nice girl."

Chapter 3.

And now abideth faith, hope,
charity, these three;
but the greatest of these is charity.
1 Corinthians 13:13

"Wake up, Stephanie."

The next thing Stephanie knew, Megan was shaking her awake.

"We have to leave in fifteen minutes."

Stephanie sat up in bed and rubbed her eyes. "Are you kidding me? It's so early. Far too early."

"Nee, I'm not kidding you. We have to leave soon."

Stephanie groaned. "It feels like I've only just gone to sleep."

Megan didn't answer. She had already left her room. Stephanie got out of bed and pulled on the same dress she had worn briefly the day before. She splashed water on her face from the large bowl on the dresser, trying to wake herself up. There was something freeing about not spending half an hour applying makeup. She was showing the world what she really looked like—flaws and all.

Minutes later, she was downstairs and ready to go. When she looked into the kitchen to see where everyone was, she saw Tara and Gretchen.

"Hello, Tara."

"Hi, Stephanie. I hear you're staying here for awhile."

"I am. You weren't here last night. I started to wait up until you got home, but then I got too tired."

"I got in late. I was out with Caleb."

"You don't have a curfew?"

"*Nee,* and don't give *Mamm* Gretchen ideas." Tara giggled.

"We only have a quick breakfast on Sundays," Gretchen explained, pretending to ignore the girls' chatter. She pointed at a bowl of cereal and mug of coffee on the table in front of her.

"Thank you." After Stephanie poured a bit of milk into the bowl and ate a couple of spoonfuls of cereal, she drank as much coffee as she could. She was hoping Jared would appear, but he was nowhere to be seen.

"Let's go," William called from the front door.

Stephanie listened to Megan's footsteps running down the stairs, and then heard Gretchen calling her name from the other room.

"I'm coming!" Stephanie yelled back before she filled her mouth with cereal.

"William hates to be kept waiting," Tara whispered to Stephanie before she made her way out of the kitchen.

Once she got to the front door of the house, she looked up at the horse and buggy waiting directly outside.

Megan said, "Oh, I nearly forgot the cookies I made yesterday. Come and help me with them, Tara please?"

As Megan and Tara hurried back to the house to get the cookies, Jared drove past in a buggy pulled by a fine looking gray horse with long silvery mane and tail.

Stephanie leaned across and watched the buggy disappear up the driveway. "Where's he going?" she asked William.

"He's going the same place as us. He likes to take his own buggy when he goes places, even if we're going too."

Megan and Tara returned with two large trays covered with white tea towels. They passed them to Gretchen and Stephanie to hold while they climbed into the buggy.

"Everyone usually brings something to eat," Megan explained when she'd settled into the buggy with the tray on her lap.

Once they were all in the buggy, William instructed the horse to move forward.

"Whose place is the meeting at today?" Stephanie knew that the meetings were held at different people's houses. There was no actual building where the services were held.

"It's at the Zooks' *haus*," Megan said. "They're an older couple with five grown *kinner* and a heap of *grosskin.*"

"Jah." Megan realized that Jeremiah Zook, one of the Zooks' *grosskinner*, might be a match for Stephanie. He was tall and handsome, too boisterous and loud for her, but he might be nice for Stephanie. He'd just come back from his *rumspringa,* so he'd be used to *Englisch* girls and because he had returned to the community, it meant that he was in the community to stay.

Not many of Megan's friend's had been on a *rumspringa.* She would never want to go and sample the *Englisch* world even though she'd not been born Amish. Besides, if she went on *rumspringa* now, what would become of her bees?

Chapter 4.

For we are saved by hope:
but hope that is seen is not hope:
for what a man seeth, why doth he yet hope for?
Romans 8:24

It was weird, almost otherworldly, to see all the Amish people arriving in their buggies. Stephanie felt like she was on a movie set. There were no cars in sight, just green fields, clear blue skies, horses and buggies, and Amish folk. Since it was a warm day, all the wooden benches were set up in rows outside the *haus*, rather than inside, as they'd been the last time Stephanie was at one of the Amish meetings.

Stephanie was ushered to a seat between Megan and Tara.

During the service, Stephanie's attention was diverted to the young men. From where she sat, she could see two nice looking ones. She'd have to wait until the meeting was over to get a closer look at them.

When Stephanie heard the bishop say the word 'mistake' amongst his ramblings, she listened to what he had to say. The bishop said that mistakes were simply a form of lesson to learn from. In essence, genuine mistakes were learning opportunities.

Stephanie found that very useful to her own situation. She could learn from what had happened to her. She had gotten caught for keeping quiet about what she knew. It wasn't fair. In hindsight, if she hadn't been arrested, she might have gotten roped into something bad if she'd seen her friends getting away with what they'd been doing.

When the bishop stopped speaking, the singing started. All the songs were sung in German and Stephanie knew it was useless to attempt to mouth the words to look like she was singing the songs.

Stephanie had to stop herself from giggling as she listened to many of the people singing off key. With no musical instruments accompanying them, the singing sounded dreadful. In contrast to the bulk of the congregation, Megan's voice was a delight. Her voice rang out clear and true like a beautiful bell resounding—every note in perfect pitch.

She looked at Megan and smiled while thinking her voice was such a waste. With a voice like that, she could go far in the normal world.

When the singing finished, Stephanie whispered to Megan, "You have such a beautiful voice."

"*Denke*," Megan said, with a polite nod of her head.

When everyone rose to their feet, Stephanie whispered to Megan again, "Do you like anyone here?"

Megan giggled. "I don't, but I've already picked one out for you. His name is Jeremiah Zook." Megan looked across to the men. "There he is, over there."

Stephanie followed her gaze. "Oh, I know him. He was a friend of one of my friends. I didn't expect to see him again." Stephanie thought it best to admit that she knew him, but not disclose the closeness of their relationship.

"It's funny that you know him. I'd heard he'd just come back from being on *rumspringa*. Is that when you met him?"

"Yes."

"Do you remember him from last time you were here?"

"Not at all." It was the truth. She'd met Jeremiah while he'd been on *rumspringa,* and had no memory of him from her visits to the community over the years.

Megan glanced back over at Jeremiah. "Do you like him?"

"Well, I don't dislike him."

"I was right. I thought you two would like each other." Megan took hold of Stephanie's arm and despite her protests, led Stephanie to Jeremiah.

Jeremiah was noticeably shaken by her appearance there amongst the Amish. "Stephanie! What are you doing here?"

"Gretchen and William Graber are my aunt and uncle. Anyway, I'm staying with them for a few weeks, possibly months."

He looked up and down at her borrowed Amish clothing. "It's nice to see you again."

Megan interrupted, "Excuse me. I'll leave you two alone; I have someone I must talk to."

Jeremiah turned around to make sure that Megan had gone.

"I told you that Gretchen and William were my aunt and uncle."

"You need to get that money back to me," he hissed.

"I don't have it." Stephanie laughed as she spoke, to make Jeremiah even more upset than he appeared to be.

"Where did it go, then? You were the only one who knew where it was."

Stephanie shrugged her shoulders. "I have no idea. Didn't the police find it?"

Jeremiah stepped in close and, with his bottom jaw jutting out, said, "What are you really doing here?"

Stephanie stood her ground and stared back into his eyes. "I'm visiting and I think I'll stay around a little longer." She walked away. It disappointed her that Jeremiah was only interested in the money. He acted like he didn't care about her one little bit.

When Stephanie reached the drinks table, she took a cup of soda and casually turned to see what Jeremiah was doing. He was leaning against a fence post, still looking directly at her with his hands casually folded across his chest. She turned away. It wasn't the reunion she'd hoped for.

What would he do with thousands of dollars anyway? It's not as if anyone actually needs money in the community. The other Amish don't seem to be driven by greed or money; I wonder why Jeremiah is.

"Stephanie, this is Benny. He's a friend of Jeremiah's," Megan said.

Stephanie jumped in fright, so lost she'd been in her thoughts. She hadn't seen Megan and the young man approach.

"Pleased to meet you, Stephanie." Benny held out his hand.

Stephanie and Benny shook hands. Benny seemed nice, but Stephanie wondered why anyone nice could be a good friend of Jeremiah's.

When evening came, the older folk went home and the young people stayed on for the 'singing.'

The young people sang songs far more lively than the ones sung during the service.

When it was close to over, Megan tugged at Stephanie's arm. "Do you mind if Jeremiah takes you home?"

Her face fell. Tara would've been going home with Caleb and that left her with no options. "Why can't we go together?"

"Benny wants to take me home. Jeremiah said he'd take you home."

By the urgent look in Megan's eyes, Stephanie could see that the buggy ride with Benny meant a great deal. If she did Megan a favor, Megan would owe her one.

Stephanie nodded, yet she did not feel safe being driven home by Jeremiah. It was clear from their earlier conversation he was annoyed with her.

When Megan left, Stephanie was worried.

"Do you want me to take you home?"

Stephanie turned to see that the kind-sounding soft voice belonged to Jared Weaver. "Thanks, Jared, but Megan already arranged for Jeremiah Zook to take me home."

Jared raised his eyebrows. "Are you sure?"

"Yes, it'll be fine." Part of her was afraid of Jeremiah and part of her still craved his approval. Maybe time alone with him would help resolve her feelings for him.

Jeremiah walked up to them and stood between them, almost elbowing Jared out of the way.

Jared did not speak to him, and simply said, "I'll see you later, Stephanie."

"Yes, I'll see you later." Stephanie could sense the tension between the two men.

As they set out for the Grabers' house, it did not take long for Jeremiah to bring up the subject of the money again.

"Tell me where it is."

"What would you do with that money anyway?" Stephanie was annoyed that he looked even more handsome to her in his Amish clothes—the white shirt and black pants— than he had in jeans.

"I could help a lot of people with that money."

She didn't believe a word of what he said. "Phooey. Those dollars are ill-gotten gains. I'm sure that's not what your God would want for you."

He shot her a quick look and then stared back at the road. "That's my business. You don't run my life, so you can't tell me what to do. I had the money and I was responsible for it. You're the only one who could've taken it. I owe other people out of that money."

"I don't know where it's gone. The police got me, and I was in jail for days until the court agreed to send me to stay with my aunt and uncle."

Jeremiah shook his head.

"Anyway, you only care about money." Stephanie tried to contain her anger.

"That's not so. You're the one who ran out on me. I didn't know where you were. I tried to find you," Jeremiah said.

"I went back to live with my parents. You obviously didn't try very hard if you tried at all. Did you confess your sins to God and the bishop for what you did—the robbery?"

Jeremiah shot her a look of disdain. "None of your business."

Stephanie hoped she was getting under his skin a little. "Well, I'm sure God wouldn't be very happy with what you've been up to."

"That's not for you to concern yourself with, Stephanie."

Stephanie looked out at the road. "This isn't the way to Megan's *haus*, is it?"

"*Nee*, I'm taking you somewhere else."

A cold shaft of fear ran down Stephanie's spine. Was he going to kill her? *Nee, of course, he won't hurt me,* she reassured herself, even though she was too scared to look at his face.

Once they were on a quiet, dark road, Jeremiah pulled the buggy off to the side. "Stephanie, I came back to the Amish because the *Englisch* way of life isn't for me. I know I got mixed in with a bad crowd, but from what I saw of the rest of it, I don't like it at all." He lowered his head. "No one really cares about each other in the *Englisch* world. In the community, everyone cares about each other and everyone helps each other out."

Which one was the real Jeremiah? The one who only cared about his money, or the one who sat next to her now talking about helping people and caring for others? She wanted the caring Jeremiah to be the real person, not the one who stole the money. Was he playing her again? Was this just another route he was taking simply to find out about the money?

Unless Jeremiah had some kind of condition which led to sudden mood swings and changes of opinion, he had to be telling her what he thought she wanted to hear. The best thing to do, she figured, was to play along with him.

Chapter 5.

Blessed is the man that trusteth in the LORD,
and whose hope the LORD is.
Jeremiah 17:7

"Can't you see the difference, Stephanie?"
Jeremiah asked now staring at her more intently.

"In the community?"

Jeremiah nodded.

"It's hard to say. I've only been here a little more
than a day. And I've only visited Gretchen and
William every few years, and only for a couple of
days at a time."

He turned his whole body to face her directly; his
soft brown eyes looked intently into hers. "I've been
a fool, Stephanie. I don't care about the money.
When I saw you again, I was shocked and said the
first silly thing that came into my head. Can we go
back to how things were between us?"

Stephanie laughed. If he was pretending that he
was interested in her to find out where the money was,
he was certainly doing a very good job of it. "Of
course, things can't go back to how they were. We
were living together for months; that certainly
wouldn't be accepted amongst the Amish, would it?"

"*Nee*, but I didn't mean that. I want you to be my girl if you decide to stay in the community."

Stephanie looked ahead onto the blackened road that was lit partially from the moonlight and partially from a distant street lamp. "It's too early to tell."

Yes, she wanted to be held in his strong arms once more, but only if she could trust him and now she knew she couldn't.

"Take all the time you need; I'm not going anywhere." He clicked the horse forward.

It was a romantic scene, clip-clopping down the deserted dark road under the moonlight, but Stephanie was not going to be sidetracked by emotion. Her head had to be clear. It hadn't been clear when she'd fallen in love with him; she had to stay focused.

A test – ahh that's it, she thought. She would find a way to prove that he loved her and was not simply after the money that he thought she still had.

When he pulled up at Gretchen's house, he tried to prolong their goodbye. To save herself from falling back under his spell, she thanked him for the ride and leaped from the buggy and hurried to the house.

After she was safely inside, she waited until she heard his buggy leave. Then she went up to Megan's room hoping she'd be home. Megan was sitting up in bed doing some needlework by the gaslight on her nightstand.

"There you are," Megan said.

"Yeah. Here I am."

"Did you enjoy your drive with Jeremiah? You took a while to get here."

"I know. It was okay." She slumped onto the edge of Megan's bed. "What's Benny's story?"

Megan smiled. "He's a friend. He's nice enough, but I like someone else."

"Were you trying to set me up with Jeremiah? Is that why you went home with Benny?"

Megan covered her mouth with her fingertips and gave a small giggle. "I thought you two might like each other. He looked at you as though he was fond of you. I could see it in his eyes."

"How would you know if someone is truly in love with you?"

"You would feel it in your stomach, or he might tell you that he loves you."

Stephanie was silent while she considered what Megan said, since Megan was a little older. "What if someone has shown he can't be trusted? How would you believe someone like that again?"

"Stephanie, are you talking of a real person?"

Stephanie was distracted by sounds of a horse outside. "Is that a buggy?"

"It's just Jared coming home."

"Megan, if I tell you something will you keep it quiet?"

Megan frowned. "I don't like knowing secrets in case someone is in danger and I have to tell."

"It's nothing like that, but I can't keep it to myself any longer and Aunt Gretchen wouldn't understand."

"Okay. What is it?"

Stephanie considered it would not matter if she told Megan all about her situation. She told her the whole story, but left out some minor details of the robbery.

"You two were in love and living together? The same Jeremiah Zook who drove you home tonight?"

Stephanie nodded. "Yeah, but now that he's back in the community, I'm guessing he wants to keep that part quiet."

"Well, I see. You think he might think you still have the money, so he's pretending to still like you and hoping you'll give it to him?"

Stephanie pouted. "When you say it like that it does sound far fetched. But, I was wondering if I might be able to test his love in some way."

Megan was quiet for a moment. "I can't see that it can possibly be done."

"Oh, I was hoping you might be able to think of something."

Megan unraveled her braids. "*Nee,* I don't think you can test someone's love."

"Well, what should I do? He says that he wants me to be his girl, but what if it's just for the money?"

"It doesn't sound right to me," Megan said, as she ran her fingers through her long hair.

"What do you mean?"

"You'd have to become Amish to be his girl now that he's back in the community. Did he mention that?"

She shook her head. "He didn't. If he did, I don't recall it. Well, he sort of implied it when he said he wanted me to be his girl if I stayed here. And another thing, he didn't come to find me and if he really loved me, he would've looked for me, wouldn't he? Even when he thought I'd taken the money, he still didn't come looking for me."

"Just wait, then. Take things slowly and let him prove himself. If it's an act, he can't play the part forever."

"You're very wise, Megan, very wise. I'm sorry we didn't get to see your bees today."

"We can see them tomorrow."

Stephanie nodded and left Megan alone and went back to her own room. Maybe it was a silly idea, making a test to see if he really loved her. Megan was right; she should just give it time and see what happens. She knew that she had been too spontaneous, too impetuous, in the past. From now on, she would wait and take her time with important decisions. If she'd taken her time back then, she most likely wouldn't have gotten mixed up with Jeremiah and his friends, and now she knew she should've left him as soon as he told her about the robbery.

Chapter 6.

He that loveth not knoweth not God;
for God is love.
1 John 4:8

"Don't you have to wear some special kind of equipment? Like a net over you and a big helmet thing?"

"I never do. They know me. I used to help the man who gave them to me." They continued walking to the beehives with the melting snow causing moisture to seep through their boots.

"Yeah, well they don't know me and I don't fancy getting bitten by any of them. Bitten, or stung, or whatever you call it. With my luck, I'll be allergic and then I'll swell up and die."

Megan laughed when Stephanie puffed out her cheeks and staggered crookedly.

"I've been stung a couple of times." Megan laughed again. "Maybe I shouldn't have told you that. You just pull the stinger out."

"Yuck! Seriously? I'm not gonna get close to them, then."

"I was joking just now. I have all the equipment to wear and enough for you too. There they are." Megan pointed to her beehives.

"I'll just watch from over here and hope they don't swarm me."

"They won't do that unless you roll around in honey first."

"All the same, I'll stay over here."

Megan waved Stephanie to come along. "They won't come out; it's too cold. They'd die if they all came out."

"Seriously?" Stephanie asked taking a step forward.

"Yes. They have to stay in the hive throughout the cold weather. Don't worry; you can come closer. If I opened it now, they'd all die because all the heat would go out of the hive."

Stephanie walked over and had a look at the hive closest to Megan.

"I've packed all the hay around the hives to insulate them and help keep them warm and keep the cold out."

"They stay there right through the winter?"

"*Jah.* The main job for them is to keep the Queen bee alive. Every hive has a queen bee. And the job of the worker bees is to surround the Queen flapping their wings to keep her warm and keep the temperature up. They live on the honey in there while they're doing that."

"Oh, that's interesting."

"*Jah*, they are interesting. I told you that. A few of them at a time will come out and fly around on a warm day, because they need to eliminate their waste, but then they'll go right back in and a few others will come out. But they won't all come out at once in the freezing cold. They are highly organized."

"What else do you have to do with them, or for them?"

"I have to give them syrup before the flowers are blooming when winter ends, when the weather warms up. If I don't do that, they could die if they didn't get enough food."

"You're brave being around them."

"They give me something to do."

"Will we come back on a warmer day and see if any come out?"

"Okay. If you want to."

"Yeah, but I'm going to keep my distance, don't you worry about that."

On the way back to the house, Stephanie thought she could see Jared in a distant field. "Is that Jared?"

Megan squinted into the distance. *"Jah."*

"What's he doing?"

"Looks like he's fixing fences."

"Let's go over and see."

Megan shook her head. *"Nee.* I'm too cold. I need to warm myself by the stove. You go if you want."

"You don't mind?"

"Nee. Go on."

Stephanie stood still on the cold ground while Megan marched back to the house, then she hurried to Jared, so she could get there before he finished the fence repair. Though not too quickly. Otherwise, he might look up and think she was overly keen to speak with him. Even though she was, she didn't want him to know that.

He looked up when she was around twenty paces away, and waved.

"Hello." She waved back.

"What are you doing out here?"

"I was taking a tour of Megan's bees."

He laughed and wiped his hands on his pants. "I don't know why she likes those bees so much."

"Yeah, me either. It's an unusual hobby to have."

"I suppose they do give her an interest and they produce honey that can be sold."

"Ah, spoken like a practical Amish man."

His hazel eyes twinkled and he grinned. "That's what I am. Being practical is a good thing."

"Sometimes it is, I guess. Anyway, what are you doing?"

"Ach. Fences always need repairing. When you finish one spot, there's always another."

"What do you do here exactly? Why did you come to live here?"

"I have no family anymore. A family in the community raised me after my parents died. They took me in." Jared chuckled. "They had five *kin,* so I guess they figured one more wouldn't make a difference. Then, as I got older, I started having a difference of opinion with some of the children. Not the parents mind you. The Zooks gave me a good life and they were caring and kind. I'm still close to them."

"That's so sad that your parents died."

Jared nodded. "I'll see 'em again some day."

"You came to live here because you were having disagreements?"

"That's about it. William must've come to hear of it because he offered me my board and keep, with a salary in exchange for farm work. He never needed a farm hand before."

"He's getting older."

"*Jah,* maybe that's it. Or, maybe he was rescuing me and giving me a place where I could be myself."

"Uncle William is kind. I can see him doing that."

He leaned against the fence post. "I remember you from a couple of years ago."

She stepped closer. "I remember you, too."

"*Jah,* It was at a singing and it was one of the hottest days I can remember."

"I was overheated and my head was aching. You noticed there was something wrong and you found

47

out I was sick from the heat and you brought me ice wrapped in a cloth to put on my head."

"You've got a good memory."

"You were my hero."

He chuckled and his gaze fell to the ground as though he was embarrassed. "I don't think I've been called anyone's hero before." Looking back up at her, he said, "I saw a girl in distress and I was just doing what anyone would do."

"No one else did it, though. It was only you. I never forgot that, or you."

"Me too." He stared at her for a moment before he looked back at his tools.

Stephanie could tell that he liked her from the way he looked at her, with just the hint of a smile around the corners of his lips.

With his head, he nodded toward the fence. "Want to learn how to mend a fence?"

Stephanie laughed. *I probably need to mend a few fences, but not fences like these.* "Yeah, I'd like to watch."

She stayed with him until he mended one stretch of fence, and then he had to leave to meet Uncle William somewhere, so Stephanie headed back to the house.

Chapter 7.

Greater love hath no man than this,
that a man lay down his life for his friends.
John 15:3

The next day.

"Stephanie, would you like to come with me while I take Tara into work in town?" Megan asked over breakfast.

"I'd love that."

Aunt Gretchen said, "And I've got a list of things I want you girls to get me from the farmers market. No need to hurry right back."

Stephanie's face beamed. "Thank you, Aunt Gretchen."

Stephanie looked down at the bacon dish her aunt had prepared. She wasn't certain what it was, and ate it all the same.

After breakfast, Stephanie went to the barn with Megan to hitch the buggy. While she was there, she looked around for Jared. She hadn't seen the place where he stayed, but she knew it was close by the barn.

"He's not here."

"What do you mean?"

"Jared's not here. He goes to work early with William."

"Oh, I didn't know I was being that obvious."

Megan said, "You weren't, but I've noticed the two of you seem to have a thing together. The way you talk to each other."

"Really? You noticed that?"

"Oh *jah*. I saw it last night at the evening meal. Now, do you know how to hitch a buggy?"

"No. Is it hard?"

"Not when you know what you're doing."

"You do it and talk me through what you're doing, and I'll watch and learn."

When the buggy was hitched to the horse, Megan asked Stephanie to go and fetch Tara who was still getting ready for work.

When Tara came out, they all got into the buggy. Megan was in the driver's seat and she headed the horse down the driveway.

Stephanie leaned over from the back seat. "Can I have a go at driving the buggy?"

Tara asked, "Have you ever driven one before?"

"No, but it looks easy enough."

"You'd have to learn all the road rules for buggies," Megan said.

"Just let me have a go down one of the back roads."

Tara turned around and looked at her. "We couldn't let you do that without asking *Onkel* William first."

"And, he'd want to teach you properly first," Megan added.

"Come on; he'll never know. I won't tell anyone."

Megan said, *"Nee.* You have to ask *Onkel* William if he'd teach you."

Stephanie slumped back into the seat and crossed her arms in front of her. These girls were no fun at all.

The rest of the trip, Stephanie remained silent while she listened to Megan and Tara talk about the dinner they were going to that night. When they arrived in town, Tara got out and then, after they'd said goodbye to her, Stephanie got into the front seat.

"Where to now?" Stephanie asked, hoping to do something fun.

"Mamm wants us to go to the farmers market."

"I know that, but isn't there something else we could do before that? Something more fun? Aunt Gretchen said we needn't hurry back."

"Like what?"

"I don't know. What do you usually do for fun?"

"I look after the bees, go to the singings, and sometimes in the summer we have volleyball games."

Stephanie folded her arms in front of her. *You've got to be kidding!*

"We could go to the café where Elizabeth works," Megan suggested.

Stephanie's face lit up. "I'd like that. Do they have caramel lattes?"

"I'm sure they would."

"Okay let's go. My father heard from Aunt Gretchen that Elizabeth just got married."

"That's right, and she married Joseph. And Tara's boyfriend is Joseph's older brother, Caleb."

Stephanie rolled her eyes. "And now you like Tara's half brother, Brandon?"

Megan giggled. "I do. I don't know if anything will ever come of it with him not being Amish."

"You're not really Amish, so what does it matter?"

"I'm not baptized yet, but I always want to stay in the community. I don't want to leave."

"I can see how that would be a problem for you. It would be easier for you to leave, though, than to expect him to come into the community. That would be a hard thing for him to do."

"I know. Maybe I'd be better off keeping away from him and not going to Tara's family dinner tonight."

"No, you must go. You might regret it if you don't. He might be your soulmate."

"I don't know if I believe in that kind of thing."

"That doesn't mean they're not real."

"Brandon's so easy to talk with. I'm not nervous around him at all, not like I am with most men. He saw right into me, like he knew who I was right away. We connected."

"That's a lovely story. I hope I find someone like that one day."

When Megan had stopped the buggy, Stephanie looked around. "Are we close by the café?"

"It's just around the corner."

Together they walked up the street, and strolled around the corner to the café.

Megan stepped back to allow Stephanie through the door first. Finding an empty table near the window, Stephanie sat down in the seat furthest from the door.

After Megan caught sight of Elizabeth and gave her a wave, she sat opposite Stephanie.

"I guess you know Elizabeth quite well since she's been with Gretchen and William for the longest?" Megan asked.

"We've met a few times over the years. I wouldn't say I know her any better than you or Tara."

Elizabeth hurried over to them and greeted them while she passed them each a menu. "What are you doing in town?"

Megan answered, "We drove Tara into work and *Mamm* wants us to get some things from the markets for her."

"Do you have caramel lattes?" Stephanie asked.

"Jah, we do."

"Goodie. I'll have a double caramel latte, please. And can I have that in a glass, not a mug?"

"Sure. What about you, Megan?"

"I'll have a lemon cheesecake and just a black coffee, thanks."

"Oh, that sounds good. Can I have a lemon cheesecake too, please?"

"Of course." Elizabeth nodded and hurried away.

Stephanie looked around at the crowded coffee shop. It was nine o'clock and it seemed they'd made it in time for the breakfast rush. "I wonder what it's like working in a place like this."

"Have you ever had a job?" Megan asked.

"No, have you?"

"Nee. But I guess I'll have to get a job soon, unless I get married."

"Elizabeth is married and she's got a job."

"A lot of women are married and have a job. Maybe my husband will want me to have a job to bring in more money."

"What kind of thing would you do?"

Megan sighed. "I wish I could just have babies and sell honey. I'd need a lot more bee hives to make enough money to matter, though."

"That sounds better than a regular job to me."

"What about you?" Megan asked.

"That's what my father's always asking me. He's sick of giving me money all the time. *You need a job,* is what he says all the time." She'd lowered her voice to imitate him, which made both girls laugh.

"You're not going to college?"

"No. I don't know what I'll do. I'm not interested in anything, so I'll just have to get some boring old job I guess."

Elizabeth brought their lemon cheesecakes to the table and set them down. "The drinks are just coming out now."

A waiter soon followed with their drinks.

After Stephanie arranged her cake and latte on the table in just the right place, she happened to look out the window to see an Amish man waiting outside the post office. "Who's that? I didn't notice him at the meeting. Is he Amish, or a Mennonite?"

Megan made a sound in the back of her throat. "That's Mark. He used to be Tara's secret boyfriend. He's not exactly trustworthy. Just when she thought they were about to get engaged, he disappeared. When he came back, he said he wanted to marry her, but then everyone kept seeing him around with another woman—Mary Lou. Now he's getting married to her."

Not liking the sound of that, Stephanie took another look at him. "Why is it always the handsome ones who are like that?"

"I don't know."

Stephanie put her fork into her lemon cheesecake and broke off a bit to taste. It melted in her mouth and the tang of the lemon perfectly complemented the smooth texture. "Wow! This is really delicious."

"I know. They make the best cheesecakes here."

"I wouldn't mind learning a bit of cooking while I'm staying at Aunt Gretchen's."

"That'll make her happy. She loves to show people how to cook."

"Yeah, but I only want to make the desserts and the sweet things."

Megan laughed. "That's a start."

Stephanie looked back out the window, now seeing a woman with Mark. She asked Megan, "Is that the woman he's going to marry?"

"Yeah, that's Mary Lou."

"They look well-suited."

"Don't say that around Tara. I think she's still angry with him."

Stephanie raised her eyebrows. "Okay. I won't even mention his name." She took a long drink of her latte. When she finished, she asked, "What's Elizabeth's husband like? I didn't see him at the meeting."

"He's lovely. He matches with Elizabeth just beautifully. His family moved here recently and I guess it was love at first sight for the both of them."

"Kind of like you and Brandon?"

Megan giggled. "Maybe. Who knows?"

"I'm going to wait up for you tonight so you can tell me all about him, and what happened."

"Would you?"

Stephanie nodded, as she now had a mouthful of cheesecake.

"Thank you. It would be nice to have someone to talk things over with. I can't talk to Gretchen about it because I told her I was going to stay in the community and then she might think I'm going to leave. I don't see much of Elizabeth now that she's married, and I can't really talk to Tara about him too much, with him being her half brother and all."

"Well then, it's a good thing I came when I did." Stephanie sipped on her latte. It had just the right amount of caramel. If only the coffee shop were closer to Aunt Gretchen's.

"I'm glad you came, Stephanie."

Stephanie liked Megan's soft and gentle nature. The downside of being so easygoing was that she might easily be taken advantage of. Maybe she could teach Megan a thing or two to protect herself.

Elizabeth appeared and pulled a chair up to the table, a glass of orange juice in her hand. "I've got a ten minute break. What are you doing today after you go to the markets?"

"Most likely chores, chores and then some more chores," Stephanie said while rolling her eyes, which made Elizabeth and Megan giggle.

On the way home later in the day after they'd been to the market, Stephanie asked, "Can we go past Jeremiah's house?"

"Why would you want to do that?"

Stephanie pouted. "Just because."

"Okay. It's not too much out of the way."

"Thank you, Megan."

Megan chuckled. "I won't even ask."

The house was set well back from the road, so there wasn't much to see.

"Looks like no one's at home," Stephanie said, gazing at the house as Megan slowed the horse to a walk. "Okay, thanks, Megan. Have you been to his house before?"

"Once or twice. Aunt Gretchen goes visiting every once in awhile and I go with her. She's a friend of Jeremiah's mother."

"That's interesting."

"Why? Are you going to ask Aunt Gretchen something about Jeremiah?"

Stephanie laughed. "No. There's nothing I want to know about him. I know all I want to know about him already." Once they were well past the house,

Stephanie asked, "And you're going to see Tara's family tonight?"

"Yes. I've been there a couple of times before. Tara has dinner with them every Tuesday. Either her father or Brandon will come and collect her and bring her home. Caleb's gone with her a couple of times, too."

"I'm excited for you."

Megan giggled. "Me too."

"Would you leave the community for him?"

"I don't even want to think about it. It probably won't come to anything."

A buggy appeared at the end of the road.

"Who's that, Megan?"

Megan squinted hard. "I think it's Jeremiah."

"Oh no. Is this the road we'd normally take?"

"No, it's not, but he won't know where we've come from."

"Don't slow down, go faster."

"If he slows, we'll have to slow too and then stop and talk. That's the way things are done on these quiet back roads."

Stephanie breathed out heavily and slumped down further in her seat. It had been a dumb idea to have Megan drive past his house.

She closed her eyes and wasn't happy when she felt the buggy slow. Opening her eyes when the buggy came to a halt, she looked over to see Jeremiah alone in his buggy.

He leaned over. "What are you two doing out this way?"

"I'm taking Stephanie out for a drive. It's such a nice day today."

Stephanie looked at him and he gave her a smile. She gave him a small smile before she looked away.

"Why don't you come inside and have something to eat?"

"Nee, denke. We've got Aunt Gretchen waiting on things we've got from the markets."

He dipped his head down keeping his gaze focused on Megan. "You're coming back from the markets?"

Megan nodded. *"Jah,* and I thought I'd show Stephanie around on the way back."

"Call in sometime. You know how *Mamm* likes to get visitors."

"I will. Err… we will," Megan gave Stephanie a sideways glance.

They said their goodbyes, and then Megan lightly slapped the reins against the horse, telling him to move.

"That was a piece of bad luck," Stephanie whispered.

"Jah, I should've realized it was around the time of the midday meal."

60

"He seemed suspicious. Like he knew we'd gone past his house deliberately." Stephanie shrugged her shoulders. "Too bad. I don't know how I ever liked him. Now I just feel as though someone else had taken over my body."

"And your mind," Megan added with a grin.

"Especially that," Stephanie said with a laugh. Megan joined in, and they giggled together as the horse clip-clopped down the road.

Chapter 8.

He delivereth me from mine enemies:
yea, thou liftest me up above those that rise up
against me:
thou hast delivered me from the violent man.
Psalm 18: 48

When five o'clock came, Megan rushed upstairs to get ready for dinner with Tara's family. Stephanie followed close behind.

"When's Tara's father coming?" Stephanie asked.

"He'll be here soon."

"Well, I guess you'll have to wear one of these horrible dresses." She touched the dresses that hung near the door.

"Yes. I'm just going to wear what I normally do. There's nothing wrong with them. I made them all myself with *Mamm's* help."

"That won't attract him."

"I don't think he thinks like that, Stephanie."

"Trust me. All men think of things like that."

"Brandon is different."

"I hope so, if you're going to wear something like that. It might be okay to wear things like that around Amish men but normal men… Well, I just don't think you should wear it."

"I have to. I've got nothing else anyway. If he's not interested in me for myself, then he's not the right man for me."

Stephanie sat on Megan's bed. "You're so confidant in who you are, Megan."

"Really?"

"You're quiet, but you know how you want things to be."

"I guess I do. I never thought of myself as confident before."

Stephanie picked up Megan's pillow and hugged it. "I think you are," Stephanie said, while thinking, *Wearing that dress you'd have to be confident.* "And what do you want to happen there with Brandon tonight?"

"What do you mean?"

"What outcome are you hoping for?"

"I'm hoping we get to have a nice talk like we do every time I go there."

Stephanie's face soured. "Talk? Is that all?"

"Well, what else could happen? I'm not sure what you mean."

"I thought you'd want him to ask you out or something, like on a date."

Megan stopped brushing her hair. "That would really complicate things."

Stephanie threw the pillow back to the top of the bed and then crossed her legs under her. "What's the point in going, then?"

"I thought you said it was a good idea."

"Yes, because you like him, but what's the point of liking him if you can't get closer to him? And the only way to do that is to go on a date with him."

Megan started braiding her hair. "I just thought I had to get to know him more."

"What's the point of that if you can't date him? I think you have to decide if you want to stay in the community or leave it."

"Nee. I wouldn't want to leave. I couldn't."

"I can tell you right now, and I don't even know the man, but he won't join the community."

"What makes you so sure?"

"It's not likely that he will. Only old people have ever joined the community, as far as I know, and they join with their family."

"I have to trust in *Gott.* If it's *Gott's* will that Brandon joins the community, then he will."

"Have you told Tara about this?"

"She knows I like him, but I don't think she knows how much. It's awkward to talk to her about him because of him being her half brother."

"I just don't want to see you being disappointed."

"That's nice of you. Don't worry; I won't be."

Stephanie kept quiet while Megan finished braiding her hair.

"You have such pretty hair and no one ever gets to see it."

"You know why we wear the *kapps*, don't you?"

"Yes, I do. I just reckon that Brandon would like to see your pretty hair."

"The man I marry will see my hair."

Stephanie had nothing to say. Megan's views were so different from her own.

"Now, what color dress should I wear?" Megan pointed to three dresses, dark green, a purple grape-color, and a brown color.

"Are they the only choices?"

"Yes."

"Oh. Well, hold them up against you."

In turn, Megan held the dresses against her.

"I'd say the purple one. The others are too dark and depressing."

"Okay."

Megan gave a little giggle and while she got changed, Stephanie looked away from the sight of Megan's boring plain white underwear.

On hearing a car, Stephanie jumped off the bed and ran to the window.

"That must be Tara's father. Wow! That's some expensive car."

"Is it? I didn't know."

Tara called out from downstairs, "Are you ready, Megan?"

Megan yelled back that she was coming. Looking back at Stephanie, she said, "I'll see you tonight and don't forget to wait up for me. I'll tell you everything."

"I will."

Stephanie followed Megan downstairs, and when Tara and Megan left the house, she walked into the kitchen to find Gretchen.

"Not many for dinner tonight," Gretchen said when she looked up to see Stephanie.

"Can I do something to help?"

"Everything's done. We're having an easy dinner tonight. We're having leftovers from what we've had the last couple of nights."

"I'll set the table, then."

"Denke. Onkel William and Jared will be here soon."

While Stephanie set the table, she said, "Jared tells me he used to live with the Zooks."

"That's right. He hasn't been here long. He'd been living with the Zooks since his parents died."

"Were his parents Amish?"

"Jah, they were. His *mudder,* Prudence, was a *gut* friend."

"I wonder why he didn't stay with the Zooks?" Stephanie was fishing to find out if Jared leaving the Zooks had something to do with Jeremiah.

"That's not your business and it's not my business."

Stephanie whipped her head around to stare at Gretchen. From the irritation in her voice, Stephanie guessed that something had gone on between Jared and the Zooks. Her best guess was a falling out with Jeremiah.

"Perhaps they'd had some kind of falling out?"

"Don't stare at me with those big brown eyes, Stephanie. I'm not gonna tell you."

Over dinner, Gretchen and William talked about the farm while Jared and Stephanie talked about what had changed in the community since Stephanie's last visit. This was not what Stephanie wanted to talk about, but there was nothing else she could say to Jared within earshot of her aunt and uncle.

Chapter 9.

O Lord, thou hast brought up my soul from the grave:
thou hast kept me alive, that I should not go down to
the pit.
Psalm 30:3

It was Brandon who'd come to collect Tara and Megan. Megan noticed that his face lit up when he learned that she was coming to dinner as well as Tara.

When they got to Tara's birth father's house, Megan was given a warm welcome from Tara's father and her younger sister, Avalon.

"Has Brandon told you about his volunteer work?" Avalon asked Megan.

"No. He hasn't mentioned it." She looked back at him. "What kind of volunteer work do you do?"

"I help out two nights a week with a van that goes around feeding the homeless."

"That's a good idea."

Redmond, Tara's birth father, explained, "It's a program our church has started."

"Before that, he worked at a helpline," Avalon said with a twinkle in her eyes.

Brandon laughed. "I much prefer the van work."

"Why? What's the helpline?" Megan asked.

"People call in if they're having a problem; mostly they're stressed about some situation that's going on in their lives. It's a big responsibility to be on the other end of those calls. Now, we've got trained professionals on the helpline. I had some training, but I'm not qualified properly in counseling. That's best left to the experts."

Megan couldn't take her eyes from Brandon. "I think it's wonderful that you give your time like that."

"It's not much really. Care to help me in the kitchen, Megan?"

"Yes, sure." Megan jumped to her feet, not needing to be asked twice.

When they reached the kitchen, he leaned over and looked into the oven briefly and then leaned against the counter. "I've made lasagna tonight and we're having it with salad."

"It smells lovely."

"I hope you like it. It's got five different cheeses and two sauces in it, and five different levels. My mother used to make it and she showed me how to make it."

"That's nice."

"I know you've told me you never knew much about your mother, but have you ever tried to find her?"

"No. I've thought about it because of Elizabeth and now Tara knowing about their parents and meeting them."

"Aren't you curious?"

"No. I guess I should be, but I'm not. I'm happy where I am now and I don't want to upset the apple cart."

"I can understand that."

"Can you?"

"Yes."

"Not many people understand me. I keep thinking that it might not turn out well for me if I met her. It's been good for Tara and Elizabeth. I just think, I'm happy now, so I figure, why going digging in the past? If she wants to find me, she can. It wouldn't be that hard for her. The other thing is, I'd be sad to learn that she died, if she has passed away. My father died when I was just a baby and she was too sick to look after me. If I found out she died..."

"I see."

Megan shrugged. "It doesn't bother me only because I do my best not to think about it. Gretchen is my mother now. She's the only foster mother who made me feel loved and like I belonged somewhere." Megan blinked back tears. There had been so many lonely days in her past.

"We certainly got a surprise to learn about Tara."

"I guess you would've."

"It makes me see my mother in a different light. She wasn't perfect after all." He gave a chuckle.

"Is that what she seemed to be—perfect?"

"She was always telling us what to do. Nothing was quite good enough. Maybe that had something to do with her missing the child she gave away."

"She was your stepmother wasn't she, Brandon?"

"Yes, but she never made me feel I was anything other than her own child. I don't remember her disappearing when I was two, when she separated from my father and had Tara. All my memories are after she came back, it seems."

"Did she have high expectations of you?"

He chuckled again. "If I got ninety eight in a test she'd ask me where I lost those two marks. Getting second was never good enough, I had to be first."

"That doesn't sound encouraging."

"It made me strive to do my best in everything, whether it was sports or school. But, it also made me feel I was never quite good enough."

"It sounds like she was doing her best to encourage you."

"I guess she was. That was her way. That might have been how she was raised."

"I notice your father says grace before every meal. Is that because you all go to church?"

"We've always gone to church. That's where Mom and Dad met."

"I didn't know that. Is church an important part of your life?"

"Very much. I put God first in everything. Would you like to come with me in the van this Friday night?"

"I'd like that very much."

"Good." He rubbed his hands together. "I'll pick you up from your house at five, and then you can come and see where we cook the food and what we do from there."

"I'd love that."

When Megan heard footsteps heading toward them, she was disappointed they were about to be interrupted. It was Avalon.

"Can't you two talk after dinner? We're all starving."

Brandon frowned at his sister. "I'm waiting for the rolls to warm."

"Sure you are," Avalon said with a cheeky smile, glancing over at Megan.

Brandon picked up a piece of celery out of the salad bowl and threw it at her. Avalon ducked out of the way just in time.

He rolled his eyes. "Teenagers."

Megan kept it quiet that she was still a teenager, although at eighteen she wasn't so very young. Perhaps he thought she might be older?

73

Megan left that night more impressed than ever with Brandon. He believed in God and even did charitable works. He was definitely a man that she could see herself with, but would someone like him want her?

When Tara and Megan arrived home, Tara went straight to bed because she had to get up for work the next morning. Megan was pleased to see that Stephanie had waited up for her, and now they headed into the kitchen.

"Well, what happened?" Stephanie asked.

"You won't believe it. He goes to church and he does things for charity. He helps the homeless."

"You've got to be kidding!"

"I'm not."

"He's like your perfect man."

"I know."

"I'm boiling water for tea."

Megan nibbled on the end of her fingernail while she followed Stephanie into the kitchen.

"So, what are you looking so worried about?"

Sitting down at the kitchen table, Megan said, "He's asked me to go with him in the van when they give the food out."

"That's good, isn't it?"

"Yes, but I'm nervous. Does that mean he likes me?"

Stephanie laughed. "Of course it does. He wouldn't bother taking you if he didn't like you."

"I guess that's right. He's collecting me from here and that's a long way out of his way. What worries me is Tara knows I'm going with him and hasn't said anything to me." Megan sighed. "What if she doesn't want me to like him? She might want someone better for him."

Stephanie raised her hands in the air. "Wait and see. Anyway, she's the one who invited you there tonight. You're just looking for things to worry about."

"Thanks. I'll trust in God and see what happens."

"Okay."

When the water boiled, Stephanie stood to make the tea.

Stephanie knew it was time to keep quiet and stop asking questions about Brandon. "Anyway, didn't you say you often had men calling 'round to see you?"

"*Jah,* you asked me that before. It seems they've stopped coming. Two came just before you got here and two others the week before that."

"Just my luck. I probably scared them away," Stephanie said as she poured the boiling water into the teapot.

Chapter 10.

For his anger endureth but a moment;
in his favour is life: weeping may endure for a night,
but joy cometh in the morning.
Psalm 30:5

When they were at another singing on that week's Thursday night, Stephanie was glad she had kept her distance from her old boyfriend, Jeremiah. He was giving attention to another girl. Was he trying to make her jealous? If so, that was a cruel way to gain her attention. It did nothing to make her want to be with him; in fact, it made her feel more distant. She pushed him out of her mind and walked over to Jared, who was heading to the food table.

He glanced over at her. "How are you enjoying your Amish vacation, Stephanie?"

"Different from what I'm used to."

Jared laughed. "I imagine it would be."

"Have you ever been on *rumspringa,* Jared?"

"Who me? *Nee,* never. I'm happy here in the community and I'd never want to be anywhere else."

"Where's your *familye?*"

Jared frowned at her. "I told you that my parents died and the Zooks took me in when I was twelve. I grew up with Jeremiah and his *bruders.*"

"Yeah, I know. I'm sorry to ask again." Stephanie glanced at Jeremiah, only to see him still speaking to the same girl. "You don't seem to care for Jeremiah too much."

Jared laughed. "Is it that obvious?"

Stephanie nodded.

"I don't like to speak ill of anyone, so I won't say anything further."

"Has he done something to you?"

"Not so much. All I'll say is that some people say one thing and do another."

Stephanie knew exactly what Jared meant. She wondered what had happened to Jared's folks, but she didn't like to ask. As Jared rolled a small sausage into a slice of bread, Stephanie took another look at him. He had a calm and assertive air about him and a confidence beyond his years, which she found appealing. Leaning over the table, Stephanie took hold of a strawberry and popped it into her mouth.

"Will the court allow you to work?"

Stephanie was a little taken aback that Jared spoke so openly about court until she realized that the Grabers had spoken of it at home, in Jared's presence. Besides, there was no one around to hear them. "I think so; there was never anything said that I couldn't work. Why do you ask?"

"No particular reason. Just wondering whether you're seeing your stay as a long one or a short one."

A smile tugged at Stephanie's lips. She looked into Jared's deep hazel eyes and knew that he was kind and trustworthy. Stephanie wondered why Megan had not thought of him as a match for her, rather than Jeremiah Zook. She would have to ask her at the very next opportunity. "Maybe long, I might stay on."

Jared smiled at her, making her feel weak at the knees.

"If you did stay, what would you miss?"

"I'd miss my caramel lattes."

He laughed. "We're allowed to drink lattes."

"I know, but Amish people live in such isolated places. At home, I'm just walking distance to a café."

"So that's it?"

"That's the main thing."

He shook his head. "You're so funny. You know you can make your own lattes."

"They never taste the same. I have two shots of caramel in the coffee and I like it in a glass instead of a mug."

"And it's better in a glass?"

"Much better. I'd better go and find Megan." Stephanie hurried away; she did not want to like anyone too much. It seemed it only led to disappointment.

As Stephanie walked through the young people to find Megan, she could feel Jeremiah's eyes were fastened upon her from wherever he was lurking. He had to have seen her speaking with Jared. She walked a few more steps and felt a warm hand on her shoulder. Turning, she saw Jeremiah.

"What were you speaking to that idiot for?"

"That's a very rude thing to say. I didn't know that the Amish were rude; I thought they were holy and nice."

"Cut the charade. You were trying to make me jealous just now."

Stephanie smiled, and said, "Think whatever you like."

"You know we're going to end up together, don't you? Tell me where the money is, and we can have a great life together. We can go anywhere, you and I."

"You're a joke." Stephanie turned on her heel and walked away as fast as she could. He wasn't serious about being back in the community. It seemed he was hiding out in the Amish community so the police wouldn't arrest him. Perhaps he'd even given the police her name to get himself off the hook.

He caught up with her. "There are things I know about you, and I can tell Jared or anyone else you might fancy. Don't think any Amish man will have anything to do with a woman with loose morals like you."

Stephanie's jaw dropped, and she covered her mouth with both hands. No one had ever said anything so horrible to her. As tears formed in her eyes, she ran into the field, away from the lively crowd.

While Stephanie walked alone in the darkness, she wondered if there was any truth in what Jeremiah had said. She had lived with him for five months as though man and wife, so wouldn't that make him just as much to blame? Hadn't he sinned to the same degree as she? She knew, from speaking with Megan, that a lot of Amish girls save their first kiss for their wedding day. She had given away a lot more than her first kiss.

She'd been too young to think of a relationship before she'd met Jeremiah. The closeness she'd had with him, the feeling of being half of a couple, was something she wanted to have again, but not with him. At least she knew now that Jeremiah was definitely not the one for her. Megan had been right when she said to wait and things would become clear over time.

Stephanie took a deep breath and wiped the last of the tears from her eyes. It had been a good thing that Jeremiah revealed his true intentions and character. Stephanie followed the noise back to the crowd she'd run away from. She hoped that no one had seen her run away crying. What a fool she was.

A familiar figure walked toward her.

"Are you alright, Stephanie?"

It was Jared.

She sniffed, and then took a deep breath. "Yes, I'm okay."

"Did Jeremiah say something to upset you?" Jared's eyes narrowed.

Stephanie dabbed at her face with the back of her hand to make sure no more tears were on her face. "Yes, he did, but I'm okay."

"Do you want me to speak with him?"

Stephanie managed a little laugh. "No, I think he's best off ignored."

"That's the same conclusion I came to a long time ago. Would you allow me to take you home?"

She looked up into Jared's kind eyes. "I'd like that."

Chapter 11.

Thou hast turned for me my mourning into dancing:
thou hast put off my sackcloth,
and girded me with gladness;
Psalm 30:11

Once Stephanie was safely home in her bedroom, Megan crept into her room. "Stephanie, did you go home with Jared?"

Stephanie nodded. "Yeah."

"Why? Is everything okay?"

"I kind of like him."

"Jared?"

"Yeah. Is that so unbelievable?"

"Nee. I suppose not. I've just always thought of him like a *bruder,* but I don't know why I didn't think of him for you before. I could see by the way he was talking to you tonight at the singing that he likes you."

"You think so?"

Megan nodded enthusiastically.

"But what about me living with a man before? Has that tainted me?"

"Nee, of course not. Everyone does wrong; you weren't raised in the community and haven't been

baptized. What do you think people who go on *rumspringa* do?"

"I suppose so."

"They get to try everything the world has to offer before they make their choice."

"I know."

"If you want to stay on in the community, confess your sins to the bishop and get baptized. *Gott* covers all your sin, and you are born anew. Now, if you were to do something like that after you were baptized, you'd be shunned."

"I see how it works. I never really knew before. Everyone seems so happy and contented in the community." *Except Jeremiah*, she thought.

"That's what the young people say when they return from *rumspringa*. No one out there cares about them like the community does."

"It's a big decision." Stephanie pursed her lips.

Megan leaned forward and touched her on the shoulder. "You don't have to make it now; you've plenty of time."

As Megan left for her own room, Stephanie knew that Megan was right, as usual.

Peace and calm floated across Stephanie as she slipped between the sheets breathing in the fresh scent of the sun-dried linen. Closing her eyes, Jared came to mind. He was nothing like Jeremiah; he would never behave toward her as Jeremiah had.

She decided if she wanted to do things correctly, she'd have to get the money back to the rightful owners since she was the only one who knew where it was hidden. To do that, she had to be careful not to get into even more trouble.

There was only one thing for it. She'd need to get Megan on board to help her since she couldn't do it on her own.

The next morning, she went with Megan to take Tara to work. On the way home, she broached the subject with Megan.

"You know how I told you that I got into trouble, Megan?"

"Jah."

"Well, some money was taken from someone and I need to get it back to them."

"Okay."

This was going to be tougher than she'd thought. "I was involved with a group of people who stole the money."

"Yeah, you told me. Did they give it back?"

"No. That's where I need your help."

Megan glanced over at Tara. "My help? What can I do?"

"I'm the only one who knows where the money is, but if anyone finds out I know, I'll be in much bigger trouble than I'm in now. I might even end up in the slammer."

"Can't you just tell the police?"

"No, Megan. You're not listening. I'll get into big trouble. It's a huge amount of money. I figure if I can get it back to the person it was stolen from, I won't need to do anything else. The pressure will be off me."

"But then the person will think you stole it and not your friends."

"I kept quiet about it and anyway, I'll give it back anonymously and no one will know who got it back to them."

"I'm not understanding everything you're saying. You weren't the actual person who stole it, but you're the only one who knows where the money is hidden?"

"Exactly. You've finally got it."

"I'm not used to hearing about crimes. It's not my fault."

When she saw Megan pouting, she knew she'd offended her. "I'm sorry, Megan. I didn't mean to be rude. Would you help me?"

"It depends. What would I have to do? Nothing bad I hope."

"No. Well, a little bad if you call trespassing bad."

Megan frowned. "Where's the money?"

"It's at the Zooks' house."

"Jeremiah's house?"

"Yes."

"What's it doing there?"

"I can't tell you that."

Megan shook her head. "I can take a pretty good guess that Jeremiah was involved somehow when he was on *rumspringa.* What's he doing with the money?"

"I told you he was. Anyway, he doesn't know he's got the money. I hid it in the house."

Megan glanced over at her again. "When were you there?"

"A while ago when Jeremiah was still on *rumspringa.* We didn't have anything to eat and it was a Sunday and he knew his parents were at the meeting. He drove over there and we took some food."

"Why didn't you just spend some of the money you had?"

"We hadn't divided it up yet, so we couldn't touch it. I didn't trust any of them and I thought they'd blame it all on me, which they did in the end. Anyway, without the money, the cops had no proof we did anything. I mean, *they* did it."

"They?"

"The other people who were involved."

"And the group trusted *you* with the money?"

"Not me. They trusted Jeremiah."

Megan shook her head. "It's hard to believe all this."

"You must, Megan because I need your help to go to the Zooks' house and get the money back."

Megan's mouth dropped open in shock. "I can't. I can't do anything dishonest. If *Mamm* and *Dat* found out, they'd be so disappointed."

"You mean Aunt Gretchen and Uncle William?"

"Jah."

"No one will find out. Won't you please help me, Megan? I'm trying to do the right thing. I'll take the money back to the rightful owner and everything will be sweet. Don't you want everything to work out well for everyone?"

Megan sighed. "I do."

"You'll be helping me if you do this."

"Okay. How do we do it?"

"We visit them and then you keep 'em busy while I go and get the money."

"Where is it hidden exactly? Wait! Don't tell me." Stephanie laughed.

Megan shook her head. "I can't believe I'm actually considering this."

"No one will find out. Besides, you're not doing anything wrong. You're helping me to right a wrong."

Megan groaned.

When they got back home, Megan knew she'd have to find a good excuse to get away from the house and to the Zooks' house. She walked into the kitchen where Gretchen was washing up.

"*Mamm,* I thought Stephanie and I might go and visit some people." She leaned in and whispered, "It might help Stephanie if she got to know some folk around here."

"*Jah.* Okay. Where were you thinking of going?"

"We thought we'd start at the Zooks' house. Mrs. Zook is so nice."

Stephanie walked into the room. "Did you say we're visiting Mrs. Zook?" Why don't we make her a cake or something?"

"That's a marvelous idea. Both of you start on the cake while I go outside and hang the washing out. I'll tell you what, I might as well come with you." Gretchen walked out the back door.

Stephanie rushed to Megan's side. "She can't come. She'll ruin everything."

"No, Stephanie. This might be good. She can help me keep Mrs. Zook occupied while you go off and get the money."

"We can't tell her."

"*Nee!* We don't have to."

Breathing out heavily Stephanie wiped her dark hair away from her face. "I dunno. This doesn't feel good."

"It'll all work out. We'll just have to hide the money somewhere once you get it. Is it big?"

"Yes! It's a lot of money." She motioned with her hands how big the bundle was.

"Well, wear something baggy and hide it in your clothes and smuggle it out that way."

Stephanie looked down at the Amish dress she was wearing. "You don't call this baggy?"

"Wear a big coat over it as well. There's a spare one hanging by the back door."

"Okay."

"Let's get started on the cake."

Chapter 12.

Blessed is that man that maketh the Lord his trust, and respecteth not the proud, nor such as turn aside to lies.
Psalm 40:4

All the way to the Zooks' Megan was worried about what Stephanie had asked her to do. It was possible that she'd get into trouble too, just by helping her. The other issue was that if she didn't help Stephanie, someone would find the money and Jeremiah and Stephanie could get into a whole heap of trouble. After weighing everything up, Megan decided she had no alternative but to help her friend.

At the Zooks', Mrs. Zook and Gretchen were busy talking while eating chocolate cake, and Megan gave Stephanie a nod indicating it was a good time for her to go and get the money from wherever she'd hidden it.

"Excuse me, Mrs. Zook, where's the bathroom?" Stephanie asked.

"It's just out to the living room and through to the end on your left. You'll see it."

Stephanie left the table, and while she was gone, a buggy pulled up at the house. It was bad timing. Mrs. Zook stood up and looked out the window.

"That's Jeremiah home. I didn't expect him home today."

Megan's heart pumped hard against her chest worried that Jeremiah might walk in and catch Megan with the stolen money.

"I might go out and say hello," Megan said standing up.

"Megan, you haven't finished your hot tea yet," Mrs. Zook said frowning.

"I don't like it too hot." And with that, Megan hurried out the front door before anyone could stop her.

Jeremiah looked over and saw her. "Hi, Megan."

"Hi there." She kept walking to him trying to think of something to say. If she engaged him in conversation, she could keep him outside long enough for Stephanie to do what she had to do. "Nice horse."

Jeremiah smiled and patted his horse. "Yeah, I like him." He looked back at her. "Since when do you like horses? I thought you only liked bees."

"Ah, you've heard about my bees?" Good! She could talk about her bees for hours.

"*Jah*. Jared told me you keep bees."

"I got the hives from Mr. Palmer. His wife made him stop looking after the bees and Gretchen thought it would be a good thing for me. I'm glad she did because I love them. I helped Mr. Palmer with them often." A mixture of boredom and confusion covered his face. He clearly wasn't a bee lover, but Megan didn't let that stop her. "Did you know that bees don't come out of their hive all winter? Except for a fly-around on a nice warm day. They keep the queen warm by flapping their wings—"

"That's really interesting, but maybe you can tell me about it another time? I've just stopped home to get something to eat and then I've got to go out again."

He started walking toward the house and seeing no sign of Stephanie, she had to stop him. "Wait!"

He turned around frowning. "What is it?"

"Why don't you come and see them sometime?"

Still frowning, he asked, "The bees?"

"Jah." She nodded enthusiastically hoping to make it seem exciting.

"What's to see? You just said they don't come out of their hive all winter."

"That's true. But you can see how I've arranged things to help keep the hive warm."

He frowned. "You want me to go and look at your beehives with you?"

"Only if you want to."

He went from frowning to smiling as he took a step closer. "How about we do something else instead?"

She hadn't planned on this. Now he thought that she liked him and had been throwing herself at him.

93

In desperation, she looked back at the house and saw Stephanie signal to her from the doorway. "Oh look. There's Stephanie."

He swung around. "Stephanie's here?"

"Jah. We came visiting with Gretchen."

He eyed her suspiciously and then turned and strode toward the house.

By the time Megan got inside, Stephanie was sitting back at the kitchen table wearing a black bulky coat.

Jeremiah greeted everyone.

"Are you cold, Megan?" Mrs. Zook asked.

"Just a little. The tea will warm me up."

Mrs. Zook looked over at Jeremiah. "I didn't know you were coming home today. I didn't cook anything for lunch."

Jeremiah pulled out a kitchen chair and sat down. "That's all right. Just give me whatever you've got."

Mrs. Zook stood up. "I can heat up some soup."

"Fine." Jeremiah folded his arms and glared at Stephanie.

"Would anyone else like some soup?"

"Nee denke. We should go now," Gretchen said.

"Denke for stopping by. I'll come to your *haus* next time."

"That'd be *gut.* Come on, girls."

The girls stood and after they'd said goodbye to Jeremiah and Mrs. Zook, they walked out the door.

Megan knew from Stephanie wearing the coat that she'd retrieved the money.

As the horse trotted up the road back to the house, Gretchen yawned. "Sitting for that long made me tired. That's why I prefer to keep doing things during the day."

"Doing things should make you tired," Stephanie said, and that set Gretchen off talking about the virtues of not being idle.

"Well, that was a nice visit. *Denke* for coming with us *Mamm.*"

Gretchen smiled over at Megan who was sitting next to her.

"We'll put the buggy away and tend to the horse," Megan said.

"Denke. I should get that washing inside. It looks as though it could rain soon." Gretchen climbed down from the buggy and made her way to the house.

When she was out of earshot, Megan asked, "Did you get it?"

"Jah. I'll have to keep it somewhere until I can get it back to the owner."

"Hide it in the barn somewhere. Make sure you hide it where no one will find it. *Dat* and Jared go in there all the time. Do that while I unhitch the buggy."

Stephanie glanced back at the house. "Okay. Any particular place you can recommend?"

"Where it won't be found."

95

"Obviously."

"No. I don't have a need to hide things. Just use your brain."

Stephanie said, "Or, should I hide it inside? Maybe keep it with me?"

"No. The barn's much better. Gretchen might go into your room to clean it. She's fanatical about not having any dust in the house. How are you going to get it back to the owner, anyway?"

"It's from a store in town."

"I won't be able to take you into town for a couple of days. Gretchen doesn't like me going into town every day. I could find some excuse."

"Okay. See what you can do."

"Quick. Go in and hide it now while you can, before Jared and *Dat* William get home."

Stephanie chuckled. *"Dat* William," she said under her breath.

Megan heard her, but she wasn't going to let Stephanie's amusement bother her. That's what she called William, and mostly she just called him *Dat.*

While Megan busied herself unhitching the buggy, Stephanie was in the barn.

"All done." Stephanie came out of the barn pulling the black coat off.

"Good. Now, I'll rub the horse down and we can have a rest."

"Yeah, but not for long if Aunt Gretchen's got anything to do with it. Idle hands are the work of the devil, or whatever she said when we were coming home."

Megan laughed. "She said, 'The devil's workshop.' We'll have a cup of hot tea first. How does that sound?"

"At least that's something to look forward to, if I can't have a latte."

"Then tonight I've got Brandon coming to take me to deliver food to the homeless."

Chapter 13.

Let all those that seek thee rejoice and be glad in thee:
let such as love thy salvation say continually,
The Lord be magnified.
Psalm 40:16

Megan got ready for her night with Brandon while listening to Stephanie's advice. Firstly, on how to wear her *kapp* and dress, and then advice on what to say to Brandon, and when to laugh. Although Megan listened and took it all in, she wasn't so sure about taking her well-intentioned advice.

"Aunt Gretchen doesn't seem to mind you going out with an *Englischer.*"

"That's because we're going to a Mission where they do charitable works. And she knows him, which helps. If he was just someone she didn't know anything about and an *Englischer* and I was going on a date with him, that would be an entirely different thing."

"Okay."

"How do I look?" Megan asked once she was fully dressed. She spun around in a circle.

"You look a bit pale. I think you need some blush."

Megan giggled. "I couldn't."

Stephanie pouted. "I don't see why not."

"He'll like me without blush, if he's going to like me in that way."

"It doesn't hurt to look as good as you can."

"This is as good as I can look," Megan said as she walked to the window. "Here he is. I can see his car."

Stephanie jumped off the bed and stood beside her and looked out the window. "Okay, well, you have a good time."

"I will."

"I'll wait up so you can tell me all about it."

"Are you sure? I might be late."

"Megan, there's no TV, no radio, no books—none that I want to read, anyway—I need my drama fix."

Megan laughed. "Okay. I'll do my best to keep you entertained when I come home."

"Good. Thank you!"

Once she was in the car and they'd greeted each other, Megan asked, "Where are we going? What town, I mean." She glanced over to see that he was wearing dark jeans and a checkered blue shirt with rolled up sleeves revealing his tanned, strong arms.

"Allentown. That's where the Mission is. It's a little over an hour away."

"I thought you would've lived closer to your father."

"He's about half an hour's drive away in the other direction. That's not too far to go for the Tuesday night dinners. We've only had these once-a-week family dinners since we discovered Tara."

"It's a nice idea to all get together."

He turned the car around. "Yeah. I know Dad misses Mom a lot. It's got to be hard for him. I think the dinners help."

"Tara said your father told her that he and your stepmother were opposites."

"Yes, and opposites attract sometimes. Not all the time, of course."

"It must be so odd for you that you never knew about Tara."

"It's taken some adjusting. Mom was always so active in the church that it's alarming that she could've kept a big secret like that. Not that I'm judging mind you. No one knows what they'd do in certain circumstances. She would've done what she thought best."

"I'm sure she did. Just as my mother did. She had no other choice."

He glanced over at her.

"I've been doing some thinking after our talk the other day and I still think I'm comfortable with not trying to find my mother. Gretchen and William are the only mother and father I've really had."

"It's hard to believe that you were never permanently adopted."

"I was sick a lot as a young child and I was told that's why I was never permanently adopted."

"What was wrong with you?"

"I had a lot of ear infections. Gretchen saw my health records and she said I got one ear infection after another. They're incredibly painful, so I cried a lot, and I was almost permanently on antibiotics. No one wants the burden of a sick child."

"It all helped to land you where you are now."

"You believe that?"

"I do."

"That's what Gretchen and William always say."

"It's fate—God's hand on you."

"Yes, but I'd use the word "grace" instead. I'm where I'm supposed to be."

He put his hand up to the air that blew out from the air conditioner. "Is it warm enough for you?"

"It's lovely and warm in the car. Warmer than the buggies."

He laughed. "I suppose it would be."

"William has a heater in his buggy, but not all of them have one."

"You seem quite happy where you are in your Amish community. Do you want to stay there forever? I'm guessing you've had to give it some thought."

"I've never seriously considered leaving because that's the only place where I've ever truly felt at home."

"That makes sense. They seem to be a private people. Closed off, almost."

"They don't want to associate with the outside world because they don't want to be tempted by things that would pull them away from God." When he didn't ask anything else, she considered that a change of subject was in order. "How long have you been helping out at the Mission?"

"My mother always used to help out at Christmas and other holidays, and when I got older, I just took on more responsibility there. I arranged the fund raising for the three vans that we deliver the food in."

"That must've been a lot of work."

He chuckled. "When I say I arranged it, I should've said that I was in charge of the committee that did the fund raising."

"Avalon said it was all your idea."

"It was, but it took an enormous amount of work from volunteers to pull it all together."

"I wouldn't have thought there would be that many homeless people around."

"I think you'd be surprised. We had a lady who lost her job and a month later she was homeless living in her car. You'd never know it to look at her. When people hear the word homeless, they think of old people wheeling a shopping trolley of their belongings around the street and when they're hungry they sift through trash—it's not always like that."

"I'm sorry to say I've never given it too much thought at all. It must feel good to help them."

"It does. We feed people on low incomes, too, and others who are confined to their homes for one reason or another. Often ill health will prevent them from working and then their standard of living rapidly slides south."

"Listening to you makes me grateful that I have a roof over my head."

"It's grounding, that's for sure. You come away knowing what's important in life."

After several minutes, he pulled into the parking lot of a large flat-roofed building that looked like some kind of a factory. "This is the Mission here. People can come here for a hot meal three nights a week."

When Megan got out of the car, he walked around to meet her. He touched her lightly on the shoulder to turn her to face where he pointed. "Those are our vans."

She nodded. "They're new."

"They are. This way." He strode toward the back of the building and she hurried to catch up.

He opened the door and immediately turned right into another room. He held the door open for her and Megan saw a commercial kitchen.

"Wow. It's huge."

"I'll show you around."

He led her around, past the deep fryer, three large ovens and a row of hotplates.

"That pizza oven over there was donated by a local man. It's worth a ton of money."

Megan nodded as they walked past several workers in aprons and hairnets who were busily preparing the food. They all happily greeted him and he introduced them to Megan. None of them took too much notice of her, but she figured it was polite of him to take the time to introduce her.

"They'll prepare meals on those trays." He pointed to segmented cardboard food trays. "Then we'll load them in cartons into the truck."

"Will I help with that?"

"Yes. You can help me pack them once the cooks fill them."

"Okay. Good."

"All the trays are recyclable, so they're not harmful to the environment. We've got a dietician who's a member of the Mission, and she's worked out the menu."

"You've thought of everything."

"I hope so. There's always room for improvement."

Brandon showed her around the rest of the building. While they were waiting for the food trays to be filled, a woman walked up to them.

"Brandon."

"Hi, Debbie." He leaned forward and kissed the woman on the cheek. "Megan, this is the dietician I was telling you about." Brandon introduced the two of them.

As Megan nodded politely at the woman, she couldn't help noticing how nice she looked in her slim-fitted jeans and figure hugging pale pink blouse. Was Brandon attracted to her? The woman was certainly smiling a lot at him.

"Megan's coming on the run with me tonight."

"Oh, in the van?"

"Yes. She'll be a good help to me since Marco is still on vacation."

"Do you need an extra pair of hands? I'm free tonight."

Megan held her breath. She didn't want to share any of her precious alone time with Brandon tonight.

"Thanks, but the two of us will manage just fine."

"Perhaps I could help you next time? Unless Megan's going to become a regular here."

"She lives too far away for that."

"Okay. It's a date then," the woman said.

He chuckled. "Thanks, Debbie, it's kind of you."

"Anytime." She flashed him a smile, and then turned and gave Megan a nod before she walked away.

"When you mentioned a dietician, I pictured an old man with gray hair. She's very attractive."

"Really? I suppose so. I hadn't really noticed."

His response pleased Megan immensely. He didn't seem like a person who would lie, and if he wasn't interested in women for their looks, he must be someone who looked deeper than surface appearances.

"Brandon, we're all done."

They turned to see one of the cooks in a white apron and black hair net waving at them.

"Good. We're coming."

Brandon and she packed the food into plastic crates that were then loaded onto trolleys. The trolleys were then wheeled to the vans. The process was repeated several times until the three vans were filled. Brandon then sent texts from his phone and four people arrived. Two to drive the other vans, and an extra helper for each van.

"You've got your list?" Brandon asked each driver who confirmed that they had.

When the two vans drove past them, Megan said, "That was impressive. Everything is highly organized."

"When we're dealing with a lot of people and hot food, it has to be. Are you all set?"

Megan nodded.

While they drove, Brandon told her more about the Mission. It was there not only to meet the physical needs of people, but also their spiritual and mental needs. They used the services of other agencies when people had specific requirements.

As Megan watched Brandon interact with all kinds of people, she grew more impressed with him.

Four hours later, they were in the van heading back to the Mission.

"One night's work, over and done. What did you think?"

"It's just a great idea. You're doing such wonderful work. It's not just about feeding people it's about being a friend. You really connected with those people."

He glanced over at her. "Exactly. That's exactly right. For some of them shut in their homes, I'm a link to the outside world."

"Everyone needs someone to talk to."

When they pulled into the parking lot, he said, "Normally, I clean the truck and unload everything from the back, but tonight I've got someone else doing that while I drive you home."

"Thank you for everything. It's been such an inspiring experience."

"It was my pleasure. I really enjoyed the night."

They climbed out of the van and he unlocked his car. "You get comfortable and I'll just drop the keys off inside."

Megan waited in the car, watching him walk into the building. She'd have another hour of him all to herself. Once he was sitting back beside her, she wanted to find out even more about him.

He started the engine and soon they were back on the main road.

"Do you live in a house or an apartment?" Megan asked.

"I live in a house. It's pretty small and it needs a lot of work. I moved into it two years ago intending to renovate, and I haven't done a thing."

"You're too busy to do anything like that, what with your job and then your work with the Mission."

"When I bought it, I thought it would be a good place to raise a family. It's got a big backyard and it's all perfectly flat. There's a huge tree that would be great to hang a swing from. There's even room for chickens and a vegetable garden."

"It sounds lovely."

"Would you like to see it sometime?"

"Yes. I would."

"I'll arrange something. Are you generally free on Saturdays?"

"I am." Since she didn't have a job, she was unoccupied most of the time apart from household chores, which were somewhat flexible, and except for the meetings.

They chatted about a lot of different things and the time passed far too quickly for Megan. He pulled up at Gretchen and William's house.

"There you go," he said.

"Thank you, again. I had a lovely time."

"It was my pleasure. I'll be in touch with you. If I don't see you, I'll send a message through Tara." He got his phone out of his pocket and scrolled through it. "Yep, I've got Tara's number which is the same as yours."

The Grabers' family phone was in the barn as they were not permitted to have one in their house.

She opened the car door. "Okay. Good night. Oh, would you like to come in?"

"No thanks. It's late. I should be getting home. Good night."

Megan closed the car door and headed to the house. She was in love, deeply in love with Brandon.

Chapter 14.

I cried unto the Lord with my voice,
and he heard me out of his holy hill. Selah.
Psalm 3:4

Earlier that same evening.

After dinner that same night, Stephanie was washing dishes when Jared came into the kitchen.

"Can I talk to you about something in private, Stephanie?"

"Sure, when?" She couldn't keep the smile from her face. Jared liked her.

"Whenever you finish with what you're doing."

"Okay. I'll only be another few minutes."

He leaned in closer and said in a low voice that William and Gretchen wouldn't hear from the living room, "I'll wait on the porch."

Stephanie nodded. As soon as he left the room, she hurried to finish the washing up as quickly as she could. Aunt Gretchen was coming back in to finish the drying, so she drained the water from the sink, wiped her hands, and hurried to see what Jared wanted.

She managed to slip outside without her aunt and uncle seeing her.

Jared was sitting on a porch chair, so she sat herself down in the chair next to him.

"It's a nice night," she said smiling up at the sky.

"Stephanie, I need to talk to you about something kind of troubling."

Looking at his worried face, she thought he might ask her if she'd been involved with Jeremiah. He wouldn't want to ask her on a date if he thought there was something between her and Jeremiah Zook.

"What's the problem?"

"I don't know how to say this, except just to say it. I found a great deal of money in the barn this afternoon."

Stephanie gasped. "You didn't tell anyone, did you?"

He frowned. "You know about it?"

"Yes. I hid it there only today. How did you find it?"

"It wasn't hard. You didn't hide it well at all. I put my hand up to steady myself when I finished rubbing the horse down and I saw a large stone. I knew it hadn't been there before and when I moved it, I saw the bundle of notes."

Stephanie sighed. "I'm giving it back to the store it was taken from."

"So this is the money you've gotten into trouble over?"

Stephanie nodded. "I had it hidden in a different place, and I just brought it back here today. If the police know I've got it, I could be in serious trouble. I was already arrested and they only let me go because they couldn't prove I'd done anything, without the money as evidence."

"What are your plans?"

"I've got to get it back to the store it was stolen from."

"How? And why did they have thirty eight thousand dollars lying around waiting to be stolen?"

"It was a store's Christmas takings. One of my friends knew someone who worked there. They keep all the money they make for the week in a safe, and then at the end of the week they put it in the bank."

Jared raised his eyebrows. "Sounds dumb. I bet they're sorry they didn't take it to the bank at the end of every day. I would guess they've been forced to change that system now."

"Someone grabbed the bag with the money in it and then ran, and then threw it to someone who was waiting in a getaway car."

"What part did you play in it? Were you one of those 'someones.'"

"I had a boyfriend and he was the one who drove the car. I didn't know anything about any of it until he came home with the money. He told me the whole story and then said he had to split it between four people. The one who thought the plan up, the one who snatched the bag, and the one who told him about the money in the first place."

"Some boyfriend that was, to get you into trouble like that."

"Yeah. I'm starting to think he told the police I had some involvement so he could get himself off the hook, too. When it had nothing to do with me. I should've just given the police all their names to start with."

"Well, I hope you're not having any more to do with him."

"No. I'm not. We've broken up."

"Good! What are your plans?" Jared asked again.

"For what?"

"You just said you need to get the money back to the store where it belongs."

Shaking her head, she said, "I haven't come up with a plan. I just thought I'd... I don't know what to do."

He grimaced.

Stephanie continued, "I guess I could leave it somewhere and call the police and tell them where it is."

"That sounds risky too. And leave it where? Someone might get it before the police get there."

"Well, what am I to do?"

He rubbed his chin. "What kind of a store is it?"

"It's a general store in town."

"I'll give it some thought and help you figure something out."

"You'll help me?"

"Yeah. I'll see what I can do. I'll take it back for you."

"No! You can't! You might get into trouble."

Jared put his finger to his mouth. "Shh. They'll hear you. I'll get into less trouble than you would if they catch you."

"Would you really do that for me?"

"Of course. We're friends, aren't we?"

Stephanie nodded. "That's why I don't want you to do it."

"I'll be okay. Trust me. I'll organize some free time at around midday, hopefully, by then we can come up with a plan." He locked eyes with her. "Meet me here tomorrow morning at six."

"Okay."

Jared nodded toward the front door. "You better get back inside."

She rose to her feet. "Are you coming in?"

"Nah. I'm more of a loner. Talking over the dinner table was enough for me."

"Okay. Good night."

He stood and pointed to the floor of the porch. "Stephanie, I'll see you here at six."

"I'll be here."

Chapter 15.

*And the Lord God said, It is not good that the man should be alone;
I will make him an help meet for him.*
Genesis 2:18

Stephanie woke up and immediately jumped out of bed to look for her watch. She thought she'd left it on the nightstand and it wasn't there. She climbed out of bed and searched around the floor. Jared said to meet her downstairs on the porch at six and since he was doing her a favor, it would be awful to stand him up. Then something caught her eye from under the bed. It was her watch. She snatched it and saw that it was fifteen minutes until six. Heaving out a relieved sigh, she stood up and changed out of her nightdress and into one of the Amish dresses that Gretchen made her wear while she was visiting.

Once she'd dressed, she looked out the window to see that Jared was steadily making his way toward the house from his sleeping quarters by the barn. As quietly as she could, she ran down the stairs to meet him.

Seeing no one in the living room, she turned the handle of the front door and stepped onto the porch closing the door softly behind her. A chilly gust of wind bit into her cheeks causing her to shiver. She hadn't stopped to put on a coat or a shawl.

"Well, what's the plan?" she asked him breathlessly.

"I've been thinking about it all night. The only thing that I can think of is if I leave it in the store somewhere and then I'll make a call to them and tell them where it is. If I made an anonymous call to the police station, they'd most likely get a recording of my voice."

"Let me do it, Jared. It's not your problem. It should be me who does it."

He shook his head. "I'll do it. I'll slip away in the middle of the day and tell William I've got an errand to run in town. It'll raise suspicion if I come and take you somewhere."

Stephanie took a deep breath. "You don't have to do this."

"Friends help each other. And you're doing something good by returning the money."

"Thank you. I feel bad for getting you involved."

"You didn't get me involved. I found the money in the barn, remember?"

"Yeah."

"Don't worry, Stephanie. It'll all work out. Give me the name of the store."

"You've got the money?"

"I've got the money hidden in the buggy already."

After she gave him the name of the store, she said, "Thank you so much. I'm so grateful."

He chuckled. "You're welcome." He wagged his finger at her. "Make sure you don't do anything like this again."

"I won't get involved with anyone crooked again, don't worry about that."

"I'm very glad to hear it."

"Be careful."

"I will. If I get caught and go to jail, just bake me a cake with a file in it." Jared chuckled as he left her there on the porch.

After she watched him disappear into the barn, she walked inside to make herself a cup of coffee to wake herself up. She hadn't had the best night's sleep, worried about what she might have to do to get the money back. It was such a relief that Jared had taken control and was looking after everything for her.

"You're up bright and early."

She swung around from the stove to see her aunt. "Yeah. I couldn't sleep, so I figured I should get up early today."

"Good. It might help if you went to bed earlier."

"I'll try that. Coffee?"

"*Jah.* I'll put *Onkel* William's breakfast on. Do you want some pancakes?"

"Yes please."

After Stephanie had made the coffee, she sat down at the kitchen table. Soon her uncle and Tara joined her, talking together as they came in.

"I'll take you to work this morning, Tara. I think Megan had a late night," William said.

"Jah, she was with Brandon at the Mission."

"It's nice to see your half brother involved in charity," Aunt Gretchen said.

"The whole family is involved in their church."

Tara looked at Stephanie. "What are you doing today?"

"I'm sure Aunt Gretchen will find a lot for me to do. And in between times, Megan is going to show me her beehives again." Stephanie took a mouthful of coffee, and then asked Tara, "How do you like working at the quilt store?"

Tara nodded. "It's good. I get to meet a lot of different people. They've got a Saturday morning job going to be available. You should apply."

"Oh no. I don't know anything about that kind of thing. Don't I have to be Amish?"

"No. The store's owned by an *Englischer,* and her two daughters sometimes work there. One of them is going off to college soon."

"What kind of work did you do when you lived away from home?" William asked her.

"I just did odd jobs here and there. Sales jobs mostly and a lot of them were cash in hand. I don't have any real experience for anything."

"Let me know if you change your mind. I could put a good word in for you. They haven't advertised the job yet and I can teach you what I know."

"Yeah, I'll definitely think about it. I guess I have to do something sooner or later."

"We should leave soon, Tara," Uncle William said, standing up from the table.

"Okay. I'm ready now." Tara stood and drained the coffee in her mug before she headed off with Uncle William.

Aunt Gretchen gathered the dishes and filled the sink to wash them. Stephanie grabbed a tea towel to dry them.

"You seem fairly friendly with Jared."

"Yes. He's very nice."

"Hmm."

"Well, you think he's nice too don't you?"

"I consider him one of the people *Gott* gave me to look after, just the same as you."

Stephanie giggled. "Yeah, well, Jared might not like to hear that you think you're looking after him. He's a grown man."

"We all need to have people we consider family. He's part of mine and I hope we're part of his. Perhaps that's a better way of putting it."

"Morning."

They turned around to see Megan yawning and stretching her hands above her head.

"Morning, sleepyhead," Stephanie said.

"Sit at the table and I'll make you some pancakes," Gretchen said. "And it's just as well you came down when you did. I was just about to wash the pan."

"Denke." Megan slumped into a chair.

While Gretchen mixed up some more pancake batter, Stephanie took over the washing up.

It was mid morning when Megan and Stephanie went for a walk in the fields.

"How did your night go with Brandon? I didn't want to ask in front of Aunt Gretchen at breakfast."

"It was wonderful. Just to see him interact with people was just so touching."

"The homeless people?"

"Yes. And everyone, really, the cooks and all."

Megan talked and talked about Brandon and how wonderful he was. As much as Stephanie tried to listen and be interested, she couldn't help being nervous about Jared taking the money back.

"You're not listening."

"Yes, I am."

Megan stared into her face. "You're not. You're commenting with the wrong things in the wrong places."

"Oh, I'm sorry. I'm happy that you like Brandon so much, but I've got a lot of worrying things on my mind."

Megan stopped walking and grabbed her arm. "What?"

Stephanie licked her lips, and decided it wouldn't hurt to tell Megan what was going on. She already knew most of it anyway. "Jared found the money in the barn."

"Stephanie! That's dreadful! Did he tell *Dat?*"

"No. He asked me about it. He had heard about the trouble I'd gotten into and figured the money had something to do with it."

"What did you say to him?"

Stephanie told her everything.

"He's going back there today?" Megan asked.

"Yes."

Megan blew out a deep breath. "That's good of him."

"I know. I feel so much better. I would've been too nervous to do anything with the money. I mean I would've done something to get it back to the owner, but I'm glad I didn't have to."

"Does he know about Jeremiah's involvement?"

"No! He doesn't get along too well with Jeremiah and I didn't want him to know that Jeremiah and I were once in a relationship. I just said it was my former boyfriend."

"Yeah. He wouldn't be too happy about that, since he likes you."

"I know."

"You'll have to tell him if things get serious between the two of you," Megan's eyebrows drew together.

"No, I won't."

"Stephanie, it'll be better if you tell him before he finds out himself. And, he will find out."

Stephanie agreed, but decided she'd delay telling him for as long as possible. "I guess you're right."

"Now I'm nervous, too. I hope he gets it back there with no trouble."

"It'll be okay. He was confident he knew what he was doing. He had it all planned out."

"Good."

"Are we checking on the bees?" Stephanie asked.

"We're just going to walk past them to see how they are."

Stephanie sighed. "Most people have a dog, do you realize that?"

"Gretchen doesn't like dogs. She was attacked by one when she was a girl."

"I didn't know."

"Yeah."

"I guess that leaves you stuck with your bees."

"It does, and I'm happy to have them."

Stephanie laughed. "I don't think I'll ever understand the attraction."

"The life of a bee is something so fascinating. Have you ever looked at the honeycomb and wondered how they get them so perfect?"

"Yeah, I admit that's pretty amazing. But it turns me off that they can sting you."

Megan started talking about how wonderful bees were while Stephanie pretended to listen, all the while worried about Jared. *He'd be at the store about now.*

Megan suddenly asked, "Exactly where did you hide the money in the barn?"

"Somewhere I'd thought no one would ever find it. I'll show you when we go back."

When they walked into the barn, Stephanie pointed to where she'd hidden the money. "I put it up there."

The phone ringing distracted them.

Megan hurried over and picked it up.

Stephanie listened in.

"You're where? Oh no! Okay."

"What is it, Megan?"

"Jared's at the police station."

Stephanie grabbed the phone from her. "Jared?"

"Yeah. Things didn't go as planned. I got caught with the money. I'm just calling to let everyone know where I am. I could be here for awhile. They allowed me a phone call."

"I'll come right down there."

"No! Stay put. There's nothing that can be done. You don't need to involve yourself further. I have to go."

The phone clicked in her ear. "Jared!" She hung up the receiver and looked over at Megan. "He's got caught taking the money back. I have to help him, and I'll have to tell Aunt Gretchen everything."

Chapter 16.

I will say of the Lord, He is my refuge and my fortress:
my God; in him will I trust.
Psalm 91:2

Stephanie ran into the house and found her aunt. "Jared's at the police station and it's all my fault."

"Did you say Jared's at the police station?"

"Yes!"

Gretchen put her hands on Stephanie's shoulders. "Slow down, and tell me everything."

Stephanie opened her mouth to speak, and Gretchen ordered her to sit down. When she was seated, she told Gretchen that Jared had offered to take the money back for her and in doing so, was caught with the money. Now he was at the police station being questioned. "So you see I have to go and tell them everything. Jared's innocent. He was only trying to help me make things better."

"How did Jared get ahold of the money?" Gretchen asked.

Stephanie cast her gaze downward.

Gretchen folded her arms in front of her chest. "It's time you told me everything. Let's go to the living room and you can tell me the whole thing and leave nothing out."

"Can we do that later? I've got to go and help Jared."

"He's not going anywhere for the moment."

They moved from the kitchen to the living room.

Stephanie sat down on the couch with Gretchen and told her aunt all about the robbery, and also told her of her involvement with Jeremiah. "You won't say anything to Jeremiah, or his parents, will you?"

"Right now, we should do what we can for Jared."

"I'll have to tell the police everything I know."

"Are you prepared to do that? They could charge you. Even though you say you didn't know about it and Jeremiah set the whole thing up, they mightn't believe you."

Stephanie wrung her hands. "I have to. It's not right that Jared is in trouble over this."

Gretchen called out for Megan to hitch the buggy.

"I'm sorry to involve you with all this, Aunt Gretchen. I've brought a big mess to your house and involved everyone."

"As long as you've learned from your mistakes. That's all we can ask for."

"Yeah, but there must be something wrong with me. Megan wouldn't have gotten into trouble like this."

"Comparing yourself with others will only lead to disappointment. Someone else could look at your good qualities and feel they fall short."

"I hope I become wise like you someday."

Gretchen raised her eyebrows. "Come on. We'll see if we can help Jared. And then we'll have to find *Onkel* William, so we can tell him where Jared is."

"Jared said that Uncle William is at the Thompsons' house today. Do you know them?"

"*Jah,* I'll call them and get a message to William not to expect Jared back today." Gretchen walked out of the house to call from the phone in the barn.

When they arrived in town and were parked close to the police station, Gretchen announced, "I'm going to have to call your parents and tell them what's going on."

"No, please don't."

"I'll have to. They'll want to know what's happening."

Stephanie sighed.

"Do they have to know right now?" Megan asked.

"*Jah,* Megan, I think it's best. I'm sorry, Stephanie, but I'm in charge of you and they'd want to know. There's a pay phone over there." Gretchen pointed across the road. "I'll call and then we'll come in and wait for you."

It was useless trying to talk Gretchen out of anything. "Okay call them, but then just wait in the buggy and if I'm not out soon, just leave. I'll make my own way home. I'll get a taxi."

"Just tell the truth, Stephanie," Megan urged.

"Yeah, I'll have to."

Stephanie walked into the police station with her heart thumping hard against her chest. Even though she hadn't committed the crime, she knew about it and had hidden the money.

She walked up to the man behind the front desk and told him she had a confession to make. He had her take a seat while he got a detective. Soon she was ushered into an interview cubicle.

Stephanie confessed everything, about how the robbery had been set up, and even how she'd hidden the money and tried to get it back to the owners. There was no other way she could get Jared off except by naming Jeremiah and his friends who were involved.

Stephanie had to make an official statement after her recorded interview was over. Four hours after arriving at the police station, she was free to leave. She knew that Aunt Gretchen would've already left, so she walked up the road intending to call a taxi from the pay phone. She could've called from the police station, but preferred to get out of there as fast as possible.

"Stephanie!"

That was Jared's voice. She turned around, hoping he wasn't mad with her.

"Jared, they let you go?"

"*Jah,* thanks to you, and what about you?"

"They aren't going to charge me. They released me a little while ago. I'd already told Gretchen and Megan to go home and said I'd wait for you. Let's go home."

"Thank you. My buggy is just up the street a little."

"I'm glad it's all over. They're going to charge Jeremiah and his friends from what I overheard."

Jared scratched the side of his face. She could see that the whole mess she'd created didn't sit well with him.

"At least you're finally in the clear. I do feel bad that they're in trouble because I wasn't successful at returning the money," Jared said.

"Don't feel like that. They shouldn't have taken it." She walked with him to his buggy. Once she'd climbed up next to him, she asked, "How did you get caught?"

He carefully moved his buggy out onto the road. "I'm not cut out to be devious, it seems."

"That's a good thing."

"I was in the store with the money and one of the workers thought I was acting suspiciously and alerted the store security guard."

"Oh no."

"Yeah. They asked what was in the bag and I told him it was stolen money that I was giving back.

The owner of the store was grateful and didn't want to call the police. The store security officer talked him into it."

"I feel so bad."

"Don't worry," Jared said. "It's over now and we're both in the clear."

"I should never have dragged you into it."

He shook his head. "It worked out for the best. It's all out in the open now."

"I bet Jeremiah will have a different opinion. The police are probably picking him up right now."

"Now that you're free and clear, no more dealings with men like Jeremiah."

Stephanie giggled. "And what kind of men should I have dealings with? Anyone in mind?"

He glanced over at her and smiled. "I might have some ideas."

"What are they?"

"Do you think you might stay on in the community?"

"I'd definitely think about it if I had something to stay for." She glanced down at his hand resting on his leg and wondered if he was going to reach for her hand. He liked her, and she knew it. Too late! Now they were turning into the Grabers' driveway.

The buggy ride was spent in awkward silence.

When they pulled up, Stephanie offered to help him unhitch the buggy.

"Would you be happy if I stayed on here for some time?" Stephanie asked.

Looking over at her, he said, "I would. I think you're too young for a boyfriend yet, but some things are worth the wait."

This wasn't what she wanted to hear. She was nearly eighteen. "I've had a boyfriend before."

He straightened up and now his face was entirely deadpan. "Tell me it wasn't Jeremiah!"

"Oh, I thought you'd figured that out."

His mouth fell open and she could feel an invisible wall come between them. "I'm sorry, Stephanie, but this is just—all too much." He turned away. "I can do all this by myself. Gretchen will be waiting inside for you. You best go and tell her you weren't charged."

She'd blown it! If only she'd never gotten involved with Jeremiah. He hadn't even been nice to her except when it suited him, and he'd dragged her into criminal activity. "Let me explain, Jared."

He straightened up and looked at her. "Okay."

She had nothing to explain. "Forget it!" She turned and walked to the house, mad with herself for being so close to having a lovely boyfriend and now it was all ruined because of Jeremiah.

Walking up the front path to the door, Stephanie kicked the small pebbles that made up the gravel. As soon as she opened the door, she was met with the worried faces of her mother and father. Behind them were her aunt and uncle, and Tara and Megan. They were all anxiously waiting to hear what had happened when all she wanted to do was be alone and cry into her pillow.

She was ushered to the living room where she told everyone the news.

When she had finished talking, Uncle William stood. "Don't doubt that you did the right thing, Stephanie. It was the only thing you could do. I'm off to the barn, if everyone will excuse me. I've got some paperwork to do."

"I don't have to go home do I?" Stephanie asked looking at her mother and father.

"You can stay," her father said.

"Yes," her mother agreed. "Just stay out of trouble. And we're proud of you for setting things right. Call us when you're ready to come home."

Her mother and father left, and Stephanie was relieved she didn't have to go home with them.

"Now, time for chores," Gretchen said steering her into the kitchen.

There were always chores!

Stephanie was too wound up to sleep that night. She wanted to be honest and do the right thing all the time, but why did she have to tell Jared the truth about her relationship with Jeremiah?

Chapter 17.

Trust in the Lord with all thine heart;
and lean not unto thine own understanding.
In all thy ways acknowledge him, and he shall direct
thy paths.
Proverbs 3:5-6

It was at the next Sunday meeting when Stephanie caught a glimpse of Jeremiah. He was heading into the house where the meeting was being held. She kept her head down, hoping he wouldn't spot her. He'd be furious that she'd squealed on him and his friends. The thing was, she'd had no other choice. It was either keep quiet and let Jared take the fall, or inform on the guilty ones who had pointed to her to save their own skins.

Throughout the service, Stephanie kept her head down. Her life was ruined. Jeremiah had led her down a wrong path and now, because she'd been involved with him, what good man would want her? Certainly not Jared, for one.

When the service was over, Stephanie was with the first lot of people who walked into the yard. Now that the weather was getting a little warmer, the yard had been set up with tables for the food and the drinks. Normally she would've stayed with Tara or Megan, but today she wanted to be alone. She spooned some kind of tomato pasta dish onto a plate and made her way to the far side of the yard and sat on a wooden seat by a tree.

After she'd finished only one mouthful, she looked up to see Jeremiah walking over to her. She looked around for an escape route, but before she could stand, he was right in front of her.

"Why did you do it?"

"What?" It was a lame response, but she just couldn't come up with anything else.

"You turned me and my friends into the police."

"I don't want to talk about it."

"I never should've trusted you."

Jared came up beside him. "Hello, Jeremiah."

"Go away, Jared! I'm talking to Stephanie about something that has nothing to do with you."

"Stephanie doesn't want to talk to you."

Jeremiah folded his arms and turned to fully face Jared. "Since when do you speak for her?"

"I'm just saying she doesn't want to speak to you."

Jeremiah looked back at Stephanie. "Tell him to get lost."

"No. Just go away, Jeremiah." Stephanie pushed past both of them and went to find Gretchen. She figured if she stayed by Gretchen, she'd be safe.

Throughout the meal, she heard whispers about Jeremiah's problems with the law. There was talk of him being out on bail and having to face court soon.

When everyone was leaving, she saw Jared in a conversation and she walked over to him. When she reached him, the man he'd been speaking with left.

"Thanks for what you did back there. Getting rid of Jeremiah."

He chuckled. "I've been waiting for an excuse to stand up to him."

"Can we be friends again?"

"We've always been friends."

She looked back at William and Gretchen to see that they were still talking and weren't leaving any time soon. "If I could take back being involved with Jeremiah in every way that I was, I would. I hope this hasn't ruined things between us."

"You're still young, Stephanie."

"You're not that old yourself."

"*Jah,* I know, but you're still learning and changing. What if we courted and then you grew out of wanting to be with me just as you grew out of Jeremiah?"

"I wouldn't."

He took his hat off and ran a hand through his hair. "You're not a member of the community."

"Not yet, but I could be."

He chuckled and stared at her for a moment. "If you join us, it'll have to be for the right reasons. The bishop questions people who want to join and you'll have to discuss your thoughts with him. Just give yourself some time. You're still young."

She nodded, figuring that was his way of telling her that he wasn't interested. If she said anything else, she'd only embarrass herself.

Chapter 18.

I will lift up mine eyes unto the hills, from whence cometh my help.
My help cometh from the Lord, which made heaven and earth.
Psalm 121:1-2

That night she thought everyone had gone to bed and, not being able to sleep, Stephanie headed downstairs.

Gretchen was sitting up, sewing by the overhead gas light. Looking up at her, she said, "Why are you looking so glum?"

Stephanie sat next to her. "Oh, that's how I feel, but I didn't know I looked that way."

"Jah. And you're completely free. The police said you weren't going to be charged. What worry could you possibly have?"

"It's nothing."

"Looks like it's something to me," Gretchen said.

"You wouldn't understand."

"Try me."

"You'll say I'm just a silly young girl and blah, blah—and all that."

Gretchen moved closer nudging her shoulder. "I was young once. I wasn't born this age."

Stephanie giggled. She couldn't imagine her Aunt Gretchen as a girl of her age. "It's nothing. It's just about someone I like."

"About a boy?"

"A man," Stephanie corrected her.

"I'm sorry. A man. Well, you can tell me."

"All right." Stephanie took a deep breath. Maybe Gretchen could have some insight. "This man I like is a little older than me. He likes me too, but he thinks I'm too young."

"Did he say that?"

"Yes. He said I changed my mind about Jeremiah, so I could just as easily change my mind about him."

"Hmmm. And is this man Amish?"

"Yes, but I'm not going to tell you who he is."

"I didn't ask. You know he can't date someone who doesn't follow the Amish ways?"

"I know that."

"Has he ever had a girlfriend?"

"I don't know. I haven't heard that he has."

"And he knows you like him?"

Stephanie nodded. "I might join the community. Who knows?"

"My advice is to carry on living and forget about him."

Stephanie narrowed her eyes. That was hardly the advice she'd been looking for.

Gretchen continued, "Don't be like that. You want him to think you've forgotten about him and if he really likes you that'll upset him and he'll come after you to make sure you still like him."

"Aunt Gretchen, you want me to play games?"

"Love's no game, Stephanie."

Stephanie giggled seeing her aunt in an entirely different light.

"Your *Onkel* William thought I was too young for him and I had dreadful trouble trying to change his mind. One day, I left him alone. I didn't look at him and didn't talk to him like I normally did."

"You ignored him?"

"Jah, and it worked. We were married six weeks later." Gretchen chuckled.

"Wow! That's a great story to tell your children. Oh, I'm sorry Aunt Gretchen."

"Don't be sorry. It's a great story to tell my niece, too." Gretchen put her arm around Stephanie. "These men give us problems sometimes, don't they?"

Stephanie relaxed her neck and let her head gently nestle into her aunt's shoulder. "They do, but now I think I've found a good one in Jared."

"Jared! You weren't going to tell me who it was."

Stephanie's mouth opened wide and she turned and looked into her aunt's face.

Gretchen's eyes crinkled at the corners. "I couldn't have picked out someone better for you and

141

I don't think you're too young. Love can find you at any age."

"I'll be eighteen soon."

"There you go."

"I'm glad I told you."

"Me too." Gretchen pushed her needlework onto the couch beside her. "Now, I must get to bed so I can wake up early to make *Onkel* William's breakfast."

"Good night, Aunt Gretchen."

Gretchen leaned over and kissed her forehead. *"Gut nacht."*

Stephanie sat alone in the living room wishing she could take back the thing she'd said to Gretchen about children. She and William had never been able to have their own, and that's why they'd taken in foster children.

After Stephanie had carefully mulled over the advice her aunt gave her, she decided that she'd put her strategy into play. It had worked for Gretchen, so it might work for her.

Chapter 19.

Cast thy burden upon the Lord, and he shall sustain thee:
he shall never suffer the righteous to be moved.
Psalm 55:22

Stephanie had ignored Jared for days. Well, not completely. She answered his questions at the dinner table, but she didn't ask him questions and neither had she gone out of her way to speak to him. The best part was, Stephanie could tell he was bothered by her lack of attention toward him.

As Gretchen and she stood to clear the plates after the evening meal was over, Jared asked, "Stephanie, are you going to the big dinner that Elizabeth's having at her place tomorrow night?"

"I'm not sure yet."

"Oh, you have to go, Stephanie. Elizabeth is having her birth mother and father there, and her sisters and Lyle Junior," Megan said.

"Yes, you have to come, Stephanie," Tara added. "You'll be able to meet my birth father, too, and my little sister and my half brother."

She looked at the three eager faces. "I guess I'll go, then. It'll be nice to meet everyone's families." She continued helping Gretchen and didn't even ask

Jared if he was going. That was part of her plan—appearing not to care whether Jared was going or not. Glancing across at him, she saw him staring at her, so she looked away quickly.

That night when everyone had gone to bed, Megan came into her room. "Are you still awake?"

"Yeah, come in."

Megan sat down on her bed and talked about how nervous she was about Brandon going to the dinner at Elizabeth's house.

"You really like him, don't you?" Stephanie asked.

"Jah. He's the one for me. Before I met him, I couldn't even talk to a man. I'd literally run away if I had to speak to a man, even in a group of people. With him, everything just flows. And he's a Christian, and he spends his free time helping the church and helping the poor."

"He's your perfect man."

"He is. He truly is."

"Why are you so nervous? It sounds like everything's going fine."

"I want him to like everyone here and I want him to join the community."

"No. I don't think it'll happen."

"You could at least try to give some encouragement or say some positive words."

"I'm sorry. Maybe I should, but I honestly don't think a man who's lived all his life outside the Amish will think it's a good idea to go back in time two hundred years to live how it was back then."

"You'd do it for Jared, wouldn't you?"

Stephanie thought for a moment. "I would, but I've grown up close to it. My father was raised Amish, don't forget, and I've been visiting Aunt Gretchen since I was little and staying here every couple of years. It's different for a man. He's got a job doesn't he?"

"Yes."

"He'd have a lot to give up. I've got nothing to lose. I don't have a job and I've got no particular skills. I'm kind of like a vagrant."

Megan sighed.

Stephanie continued, "What if he wanted you to leave the community? Would it be so bad? Would your life be that bad? He's involved in his church and you could do the charity work together. Someone would look after your bees. Not me, but someone would care for them."

Megan said in a small voice, "I hadn't even thought about my bees."

"Whatever will happen will happen. Don't worry about it. Don't let him go if he asks you to marry him. You must say yes and figure things out later."

Megan slowly nodded. "I don't know if he's even thinking of me in that kind of a way."

"He asked you to go to the homeless shelter with him, didn't he?"

"It wasn't a homeless shelter, but yes, he asked me to go with him in the van to make the deliveries, and I saw how they prepared the food. He showed me around the Mission and he even asked me if I wanted to come and see his house sometime."

"See? He wouldn't have bothered with all that if he didn't like you."

"I hope you're right. I feel in my heart that he likes me, but I've never had a man in my life, so I can't trust in my feelings."

"I'll watch him with you tomorrow night and I'll tell you what I think."

"Would you?"

"Yeah."

The next night, Jared went alone in his buggy while Tara, Megan and Stephanie went with Gretchen and William.

While they traveled, Tara explained how Elizabeth's father found her in a coffee shop and thought she looked like one of his daughters, not knowing that she *was* his daughter. The more Stephanie listened to how everything unfolded she learned how unsettling it was for Gretchen's foster girls not to be acquainted with their birth parents. Her mind drifted to her own upbringing. She hadn't been the easiest child to handle growing up and she regretted what she'd put her parents through. *It's no wonder they kept sending me to stay with Aunt Gretchen and Uncle William.*

Uncle William pulled up the buggy outside the house alongside a row of buggies. Closer to the house were three cars.

"It looks like everyone's here already," Gretchen said as she climbed down from the buggy.

As they walked to the house, Jared joined them, having just pulled up in his own buggy.

"Stephanie, can I speak to you a moment?" Jared asked.

Stephanie stopped while the others continued to the house.

"What is it?" she asked sweetly.

"I've noticed you've been acting a little different toward me and I'm wondering if I've done something to offend you."

"No. You've done nothing. You helped me with that money and everything, and I'm really grateful for that."

"Nothing's wrong?"

She shook her head. "Nothing."

He looked down at the ground and then stared into her face. "Would you like to come home in my buggy with me tonight when we finish here?"

Stephanie could barely keep the smile from her face. She wanted to leap high in the sky and give a couple of hollers, but she restrained herself. "I'd like that."

A smile slowly spread across his face. "Good." He looked at the house. "We better get inside."

She walked with him into the house, pleased that Gretchen's advice had actually worked and it hadn't taken too long.

Chapter 20.

The Lord is my strength and my shield;
my heart trusted in him, and I am helped:
therefore my heart greatly rejoiceth;
and with my song will I praise him.
Psalm 28:7

When Megan was inside Elizabeth's house, she scanned the room everywhere looking for Brandon. He was nowhere to be seen. She said hello to the rest of Tara's family and then to Elizabeth's family members that she'd met at the wedding. Her heart thumped hard when she heard another car pull up outside, hoping it would be Brandon.

A few minutes later, there he was at the doorway. Tara raced over toward him and introduced him to everyone. When the introductions were over, he looked across the room and smiled at Megan and then made his way to her.

"Hello."

"Hi. I thought you mightn't be coming," Megan said.

"I wanted to meet some of your friends and Tara's friends. I've already met Gretchen and William."

Brandon had often collected Tara and taken her to the Tuesday night family dinners. It was on one of those occasions that he'd met William and Gretchen.

"I really liked going with you in the van the other night."

He laughed. "I've been thinking about that. It wasn't a good choice for a place to take you."

"Oh, it was."

"I was thinking that I should take you out somewhere properly, like out to dinner if you'd be interested."

"That sounds good to me."

"Okay. How about tomorrow night?"

"Tomorrow?"

"Too soon?" he asked leaning toward her.

"No. I think tomorrow would be just fine."

At that moment, Megan knew that Brandon liked her just as she liked him. Relief was what she felt. "I should see if Elizabeth wants some help in the kitchen."

She was nervous around him for the first time and she thought she hid it rather well. Brandon hadn't mentioned her seeing his house, but going on an actual date was even more of a step forward.

Walking into the kitchen, she saw that Elizabeth had everything under control. The food was already lined up on platters along the long wooden table.

Nerves and excitement would prevent her from eating anything at all that night.

"Have you seen what we've done to the *haus*, Megan?" Elizabeth asked.

"Nee. I haven't."

"I'll show you around if you want to see."

"Of course, I do."

"We'll start upstairs."

"Now? Isn't dinner about to start?"

"Not yet. We're waiting on a couple more people. Come on."

When they got upstairs, Elizabeth pulled her into her bedroom and flopped down on the bed. "That was just an excuse to have a rest."

Megan giggled. "Your family seems nice."

"Most of them are. I'm still not close to my father's mother yet. My parents wanted to buy me furniture, but Joseph said we shouldn't accept. I suppose he's right. He wants us to do everything on our own."

"His parents gave him this *haus,* though."

"One thing you'll find is that men don't make much sense. It seems that we can take a helping hand from his family, and not from mine."

"Ah, I see. His are in the community and yours are not?" Megan inquired.

Elizabeth nodded. "Possibly that's it."

"Do you like being married?"

"I do. It's one of the best things to have happened to me. Sit down now, and tell me everything that's been going on with you."

Megan sat down on the bed and was glad to tell her about Brandon. "Well, what do you think? He's not in the community, and Stephanie thinks he'll never join."

"Have you asked him?"

"Nee. He might think I'm rushing things if I ask him that."

"You need to know everything upfront, Megan. You don't want to waste your time with him if he's not going to be a part of our family."

Megan knew Elizabeth was referring to the larger family of the community.

Elizabeth continued, "You'll save yourself a lot of heartache if you get that out of the way before you get too involved with him."

"You think?"

"Jah. I do. In fact, I know it."

Megan sighed. "I guess you're right. He asked me to dinner, so I'll talk with him about it then."

"Perfect. Now let's go downstairs and get this meal started. If the other guests haven't arrived, too bad. Everyone's hungry."

When the night was over, Jared walked up beside Stephanie as she was helping Elizabeth finish up in the kitchen.

"Let me know when you're ready to go, Stephanie."

"You can go now, Stephanie. Thanks for your help. You didn't have to work so hard. You were supposed to be enjoying yourself. There's not much to do now," Elizabeth said trying to keep the smile from her face.

Stephanie had been putting her best foot forward. She knew that Jared would want her to be helpful to others.

Gretchen and William had left minutes earlier, and Brandon had taken Megan home, and Tara had left with Caleb.

"Are you sure?" Stephanie asked.

"Of course. *Denke* for coming." Elizabeth glanced over at Jared. "Both of you."

He smiled. *"Denke* for a lovely dinner, Elizabeth. It was nice to meet your family."

When Stephanie walked outside, she shivered in the cold night air.

"Do you want my coat?" Jared asked.

"I'll be okay. It's not far to the buggy."

As they walked, he said, "I hope I didn't offend you by anything I said the other day about your age."

"You could never do that."

"I mean you're not that young."

"I know that. I was waiting for you to realize it."

When they pulled up at the house, he said, "Go into the kitchen and I'll be there in about fifteen minutes. I've got a surprise for you."

"Really?" Stephanie loved surprises.

"Jah. Don't look so shocked."

She laughed. "Okay. I'll be waiting." When she was inside, she was pleased to see no one in the kitchen. She would be able to have some private time with Jared.

Chapter 21.

I cried unto the Lord with my voice,
and he heard me out of his holy hill. Selah.
Psalm 3:4

Several more minutes, Jared poked his head through the back door.

"Come in," Stephanie said.

"Is it safe?"

"We're alone."

He pushed the door open and he had something in his hands.

"What's that?"

He placed it down in front of her. "This is your double caramel latte."

"You remembered?" She stared at the hot drink in the glass.

"Yes."

"You made it just for me?"

"I did. I've been practicing to get them just right. Taste it."

She picked it up and took a sip. "Mmm. It's excellent! Just the way I like them, and it's in a glass. I can't believe you've done this for me."

"Well, I did. And I've got a few things to tell you." He settled down in front of her.

"What?"

"To start with, I'll have to go back to when I first saw you a couple of years ago. I liked you back then and I never forgot you."

She resisted the urge to tell him she felt the same.

He continued, "I made the mistake of telling Jeremiah I liked you. You obviously don't remember him from your visit to the community two years ago, but I can tell you that he must've known who you were when he met you on his *rumspringa.*"

"Really?"

"That's right. We were friends once, but a year ago things soured between us, just before he left."

"What happened?"

"Just a series of small things. I get along with everyone else in the family except for him."

"Do you think he only got involved with me to get back at you?"

"I'm not saying that. Who wouldn't want you as a girlfriend?"

"You?"

He shook his head and touched the glass of latte. "I made this to show you that there'll be nothing you'll miss if you'll join the community. I can make you as many of these as you want. Six a day isn't too many."

She laughed. "You want me to?"

"I've always wanted you to. I just was worried that you might not be ready, or that you might be too young to make a decision for the rest of your life." He reached out and took hold of her hand. "I had to tell you how I feel. You've been on my mind since the last time you were here. I hoped you'd be back and here you are."

She looked away from him. "I feel like a fool for being involved with Jeremiah and the whole robbery thing."

"Forget it. You wouldn't be human if you didn't make a mistake."

"Doesn't it bother you?"

He chuckled. "It doesn't make me happy, but *you* do. I don't want to put pressure on you, but I couldn't risk you leaving again without me telling you how I feel. When do you turn eighteen?"

"In three months."

He closed his eyes for a moment, and when he opened them, he said, "Would you marry me? You'd have to join the community."

"Yes, I will."

He reached out and took her hand. "If you feel the same when you turn eighteen, we'll marry the day after."

She giggled. "I'll feel the same."

"Are you sure? This is a serious life long decision."

"I do. I'll definitely feel the same. I've always remembered you too, from the last time I was here."

When they heard a car pull up outside, Jared said, "I should go."

"What shall we tell everyone?"

"They'll figure it out soon enough, when you spend every moment with me."

She looked into his deep hazel eyes and he smiled as he squeezed her hand. Before he rose to his feet, he leaned over and kissed her on her forehead.

They heard the front door close.

"That sounds like Megan has come home."

"Good night, Stephanie. I'll see you after work tomorrow and we'll do something together."

"Okay. Good night."

After he had left, Stephanie looked at the latte. She sipped it, but it had gone lukewarm.

* * *

Minutes earlier.

When Megan got in Brandon's car to go home, Elizabeth's words played on her mind. She could feel herself falling in love with Brandon, and she had to know where he stood about things and what he was thinking. She cleared her throat and began the conversation as he pulled his car out of Elizabeth's driveway on the way to take her home. He glanced over at her as though he knew she had something to say.

"Brandon, I'm wondering what you think about the Amish."

He laughed. "I've always been charmed and fascinated by the lifestyle."

"You have?"

"It's a simple way of life with no distractions everyone helping each other and living in a real community. I've often wondered if I could do it."

"Live in the community you mean?"

"Yes, that's what I mean. I've never had any serious thoughts about it before I met you just thoughts in passing."

"So, what you're saying is — "

"What I'm saying to you is that if things progress in the right way between us, I will look into joining your community."

"Really?"

"Sure. Will I still be able to do my charity work?"

"The Mission would be too far to travel to in the buggy, but you could do other charity work closer to home."

He nodded. "I'm glad we had this conversation that tells me that you're a woman who is straightforward and I like that."

She smiled and looked at the dark road ahead grateful that Elizabeth had prodded her into talk to him to gauge his intentions.

"Is your bishop available for an outsider like me to have a conversation with?"

"Yes, of course, he is."

"Well, I think that's something I'd like to do soon."

When he stopped the car outside her house, he turned off the engine. "Don't go just yet."

She removed her hand from the door handle and looked at him.

"I want you to know that I'm serious about you, Megan. I know we've only just met, but I know we're heading in a good direction. I'm not passing the time with you. That's not why I've wanted to spend time with you. I think you and I have a future together."

She smiled at him. That's all she'd wanted to know. Now that he said he'd consider joining the community and was going to speak to the bishop, she couldn't ask for better news.

"Thank you for letting me know how you feel. I've been thinking the same things."

"Good. I'll see you soon." He leaned over and gave her a quick kiss on the cheek.

Her body tingled at the feel of his lips, and she wanted to feel his arms around her and kiss him properly. All that would come in time.

"Bye, Brandon."

"Good night, Megan." She opened the car door and hurried into the house.

"Are you still awake?"

Stephanie turned around and saw Megan walking into the kitchen.

"Yeah," Stephanie answered.

"Where did you get that?" Megan looked at the latte as she sat down.

"Jared made it for me." Stephanie couldn't keep the smile from her face. "He wants to marry me."

"What?"

"Jared wants to marry me."

Megan laughed. "I heard. I'm just surprised. Stephanie, that's wonderful news and so sudden. I've got some good news, too."

"What is it?"

"Tonight, Brandon and I had a talk. He said he's not against the idea of joining the community, but he'd have to find out more. He's actually going to talk with the bishop."

Stephanie leaped out of her chair and hugged Megan. "Megan, I'm so happy for you!"

"I'm happy for you too. It's not for certain with Brandon, and I don't know what's going to happen in the future, but I feel confident. I know he's the man for me and *Gott* will make a way for us to be together. Just like he made a way for you and Jared."

Sitting back down, Stephanie remembered her prayer when she first arrived at Aunt Gretchen's house. Also, she thought back to her recent talk with her aunt; Aunt Gretchen had said that love could find her at any age, and it had.

Thou hast turned for me my mourning into dancing:
thou hast put off my sackcloth,
and girded me with gladness;
Psalm 30:11

Thank you for your interest in
The New Amish Girl

To be notified of Samantha Price's New Releases,
add your email at her website:
www.samanthapriceauthor.com

Books in the Amish Foster Girls series:

Other books by Samantha Price:
AMISH LOVE BLOOMS

EXPECTANT AMISH WIDOWS

ETTIE SMITH AMISH MYSTERIES (Cozy Mystery series)

AMISH BABY COLLECTION

AMISH BRIDES

AMISH SISTERS
Book 1 Amish Trading Places
Book 2 Amish Truth Be Told
Book 3 The Big Beautiful Amish Woman
Book 4 The Amish Widow and the Millionaire

AMISH MAIDS
Book 1 The Amish Nanny
Book 2 The Amish Maid
Book 3 A Rare Amish Maid
Book 4 In My Sister's Shadow
Book 5 Change of Heart
Book 6 Game of Love
Book 7 Amish Life of Lies

AMISH ROMANCE SECRETS
Book 1 A Simple Choice
Book 2 Annie's Faith
Book 3 A Small Secret
Book 4 Ephraim's Chance
Book 5 A Second Chance
Book 6 Choosing Amish

AMISH WEDDING SEASON
Book 1 Impossible Love
Book 2 Love at First
Book 3 Faith's Love
Book 4 The Trials of Mrs. Fisher
Book 5 A Simple Change

AMISH SECRET WIDOWS' SOCIETY (Cozy
Mystery Series)
Book 1 The Amish Widow
Book 2 Hidden
Book 3 Accused
Book 4 Amish Regrets
Book 5 Amish House of Secrets
Book 6 Amish Undercover
Book 7 Amish Breaking Point
Book 8 Plain Murder
Book 9 Plain Wrong
Book 10 Amish Mystery: That Which Was Lost

WESTERN MAIL ORDER BRIDES
Book 1 Mail Order Bride: Deception
Book 2 Mail Order Bride: Second Choice
Book 3 Mail Order Bride: Revenge
Book 4 Widowed and Expecting: Mail Order Bride
Book 5 Mail Order Bride: Too Good For The Doctor

WILD WEST FRONTIER BABIES
Book 1 Mail Order Bride: The Rancher's Secret Baby
Book 2 The Nursemaid's Secret Baby

Stand Alone Novella:
Marry by Christmas (Western Romance)

Samantha Price loves to hear from her readers.
Connect with Samantha at:

samanthaprice333@gmail.com
www.twitter.com/AmishRomance
www.samanthapriceauthor.com
www.facebook.com/SamanthaPriceAuthor

44442876R00095

Made in the USA
Middletown, DE
06 June 2017